The Skipworth Summer

I promised myself I would never go back. But then, I've broken promises before. Fortified by the enthusiasm of my ninth graders (*Mr. Benedict, Dude, you should SO go*), I packed an overnighter, gassed up the Nova, and headed north.

Highway 7 west of Little Rock through Jasper is a little piece of motor-head heaven. The views are incredible and the road fun to drive. Those winding bends never reveal what's ahead, and then suddenly you're practically meeting yourself on a tight, hairpin turn. I took my time, stopping briefly in Harrison before making my way into Berryville and that little corner building on Church Street.

Skip's is no longer there, of course. I've heard the building has housed everything from an antiques store to a bait shop over the years. It's a tea room now, but I'm betting it won't last. Nothing does. The Wal-Mart Supercenter on the north edge of town has sapped the flavor from the old town square. Even so, I could still make out the faded mural painted on the side of the old barber shop. I ran my hand along the rough bricks, then walked around to the glass front and tried to peer in. The place was closed and the dark impenetrable. When I stepped back, though, I could see my reflection in the glass. Whether it was a trick of light from the afternoon sun or just a wave of nostalgia, the years seemed to slip away, and I was just a frightened fifteen-year-old kid with a chip on my shoulder. I looked down at my hands, expecting...

The Skipworth Summer

by

Jan Netolicky

A Wings ePress, Inc.

Young Adult Novel

Wings ePress, Inc.

Edited by: Cherri Jetton
Copy Edited by: Joan Powell
Senior Editor: Anita York
Executive Editor: Marilyn Kapp
Cover Artist: Pat Evans

All rights reserved

Names, characters and incidents depicted in this book are products of the author's imagination or are used fictitiously. Any resemblance to actual events, locales, organizations, or persons, living or dead, is entirely coincidental and beyond the intent of the author or the publisher.

No part of this book may be reproduced or transmitted in any form or by any means, electronic or mechanical, including photocopying, recording, or by any information storage and retrieval system, without permission in writing from the publisher.

Wings ePress Books
http://www.wings-press.com

Copyright © 2012 by Jan Netolicky
ISBN 978-1-61309-953-7

Published In the United States Of America

February 2012

Wings ePress Inc.
403 Wallace Court
Richmond, KY 40475

Dedication

For Gus, Sophia, and Max

Prologue

Looking Glass, Present Day

I promised myself I would never go back. But then, I've broken promises before. Fortified by the enthusiasm of my ninth graders (*Mr. Benedict, Dude, you should SO go*), I packed an overnighter, gassed up the Nova, and headed north.

Highway 7 west of Little Rock through Jasper is a little piece of motor-head heaven. The views are incredible and the road fun to drive. Those winding bends never reveal what's ahead, and then suddenly you're practically meeting yourself on a tight, hairpin turn. I took my time, stopping briefly in Harrison before making my way into Berryville and that little corner building on Church Street.

Skip's is no longer there, of course. I've heard the building has housed everything from an antiques store to a bait shop over the years. It's a tea room now, but I'm betting it won't last. Nothing does. The Wal-Mart Supercenter on the north edge of town has sapped the flavor from the old town square. Even so, I could still make out the faded mural painted on the side of the old barber shop. I ran my hand along the rough bricks, then walked around to the glass front and tried to peer in. The place was closed and the dark impenetrable. When I stepped back, though, I could see my reflection in the glass. Whether it was a trick of light from the afternoon sun or just a wave of nostalgia, the years seemed to slip away, and I was just a frightened fifteen-year-old kid with a chip on my shoulder. I looked down at my hands, expecting…

One

Caught Red-Handed

1975

My hands were stained red once before. Only then, the stains weren't blood. They were indelible red ink.

Bo gave me the idea. He was always thinking of ways to cause trouble, but K.D., Major, and I put the plans in motion. We were in town that Saturday on leave from the county boys' school. Believe me, I use the term "town" loosely. Berryville, Arkansas, is not exactly the Las Vegas hot spot of the South. Anyway, Bo thought we ought to paint the town red—literally. We figured a gallon of bright crimson enamel and four brushes were beyond our financial means, and even though we'd had some experience in the delinquency department, defacing public property in broad daylight would be a little tricky.

So we opted for the subtle approach. I had seen Charlton Heston play Moses in *The Ten Commandments.* My favorite scene was when he turned the waters of the Nile blood red with a touch of his staff. The fountain in the middle of the town square was definitely not the Nile, and five bottles of red ink from the Berryville Drug wasn't the blood of a persecuted people, but the effect on the local yokels was about as dramatic as it had been on Egyptian royalty. I sat nonchalantly on the edge of the limestone, emptied the bottles into the water and waited.

Fred Kirkpatrick was the first to notice the Technicolor treatment of the fountain. He was on his lunch break from his job as the county auditor. Every work day he ate his lunch on the bench facing the courthouse, like some Islamic disciple bowing to Mecca. When he saw that red ink drifting toward the pump in the fountain, Fred almost passed out. Probably nothing since the last county election, when he defeated Clara Matthews by a thirteen-vote margin, had caused him such agitation.

Waving his arms and shouting frantically, Fred finally caught Sheriff Stoner's attention. Berryville's one-man law force left the comfort of his squad car and strolled over to Fred, who was gesturing helplessly toward the fountain. By this time, pink water was gurgling into the lower basin.

With no help from Fred, Sheriff Stoner sized up the situation. Although the guys and I had long since vamoosed to the corner booth at the Berryville Drug, Stoner was like a bloodhound. He found us eating potato chips and drinking Dr. Peppers and trying to keep straight faces.

"Okay, buzzards. Who's the wiseass?" Stoner demanded.

"Sir?" D.J. snickered.

"Who dyed the water in the fountain?"

"Give a guy a break, sheriff. We've just been relaxing. You know we like to make the most of our Saturday visits, sir." D.J.'s inflection made the "sir" sound like a four-letter word.

"Oh, yeah. I got it," snorted Stoner. "And you get this. I'm through with the lot of you. So help me God, I'll get the county attorney to issue an injunction to keep you and the rest of the creeps at that school permanently. If that doesn't work, I swear I'll look the other way when the people of this town get a craw full of you low-lifes and take matters into their own hands."

Big deal, I thought. The sheriff had no proof. Nobody had actually seen me dump the ink, and even if someone had noticed a dark-haired kid perched on the edge of the fountain, so what? Berryville kids met at the center of town all the time to hang out, especially on the weekends, and there wasn't much to distinguish me from them. I may have been a little scrawnier than other fifteen-year-old guys, but because I don't *look* too intimidating, that probably works to my advantage. That, and my best feature—hazel-colored eyes that seem to disarm people. I've been told when people look me in the eye, they'd believe me if I said I was President Ford. Trust me, I wouldn't be the first guy picked out of a lineup, and that ain't bad. Without an eyewitness who could mark me as guilty, Sheriff Stoner couldn't do a thing. The smirk on my face must have irritated him something fierce.

He slammed a fist on the table in front of me and shoved his big ugly face in front of Major. "Go ahead and laugh, scumbags. I'll see to it you're processed in my jurisdiction instead of Eureka. We'll quit screwing around with this kid glove treatment."

It was an empty threat, but something spooked Major. I knew he was a big talker, but when the pinch was on, he usually was out to save his own skin. "I swear I didn't know what he was going to do," he mumbled.

Stoner pounced. "Okay, spill it, moron." He was practically spitting at Major.

K.D. and Bo kept quiet. I knew they would have stuck by me even if Stoner shoved bamboo under their nails. But the sheriff wasn't going anywhere. Not this time. I had to set things straight before Major had a coronary. Technically, the ink was mine and so was the responsibility. Besides, we were drawing quite an audience, including dark-eyed Sara Greenwoldt who worked behind the lunch counter. Might as well play this to the hilt.

I raised my hands—only slightly ink-stained—

dramatically in the air, rose from the booth, and swaggered toward the door. On a whim, I winked at Sara. She blushed and pretended to look busy, but I think she thought I was holding my own with Stoner.

"Figures," Stoner observed. "In a hole of skunks, Benedict, your stench is the strongest. Let's go, punk." He barked at the trio still seated in the booth. "You three hightail it back to the school. I'll have my secretary call the head man with a full report. Don't let me catch you back here again. You show your faces, you win a one-way ticket to the state correctional farm. Got it?"

K.D. and Bo stood by the door, deliberately ignoring Major. Nodding to the two of them, I left with Stoner close behind me. I kept my hands in the air until we were out of Sara's line of vision. Then, somehow, the whole charade just didn't seem worth the effort anymore.

Two

A Chance Meeting

Sheriff Stoner and I headed for the courthouse on the opposite side of the town square. Even though my prospects didn't look so hot at the moment, I knew Major was in for much rougher treatment when he got back to school. K.D. and Bo would waste no time labeling him as a snitch. Major was going to have an accident—maybe a slip on the stairs or an ankle broken in a pickup game of basketball—bad enough to lay him up for at least a couple of weeks in the infirmary. If K.D. and Bo were implicated, they could still be sent to the reformatory. Our lives were steamrolling downhill without any brakes. The speeds might differ a little, but we were all going to crash at the bottom.

The four of us had met at The Cedars, officially known as the county home for orphaned and delinquent boys, but those of us who lived there called it "Loser Central." Most of us were wards of the state. Most of us had come up the same way. I think Major was sent to The Cedars when he was nine. His father, a decent guy, had been hurt in an accident on their farm outside Alpena. He was caught in a mower and badly mangled, but he didn't die right away. He hung on long enough to build up unpayable hospital bills and to give Major's mom an excuse to drink herself senseless. Major stayed with his grandparents for a time, but they really weren't able to manage the responsibility. Somewhere along the line, Major's mom was committed to an institution to dry out. By then, Major was already thirteen, too old to be wanted by adoptive parents. His future at The Cedars was sealed. Even though he had messed me up with Stoner, I still felt kind of sorry for him.

The rest of the stories were about the same. Some of the other guys were victims of separation or divorce, child abuse, accidents, drugs, you name it. Some, like me, were unwanted even before they were born. I guess my mother was unmarried and only just turned seventeen when she had me. Even if she had been married and my birth had been more than an accident, she probably would have given me up for adoption anyway. I'm not one to inspire motherly affection, I guess. Maybe I cried all the time when I was little. That can be as annoying as hell. Maybe I acted all psycho, like some demon baby. Who knows? I sure never got the chance to ask dear old Mom why she didn't want me. And when she handed me over to Child Welfare, that was just the beginning. Whatever the reason, I was bounced around in foster care for several years before landing at Loser Central when I was ten. Not one of my seven foster families even entertained the notion of adopting me.

Sheriff Stoner interrupted my silent thoughts. "What's the matter, Benedict? Not such a smart-ass hot shot without an audience, are you?"

I shrugged. For once, Stoner was right.

We entered the courthouse and made our way to his office on the second floor. I know this sounds corny, given the circumstances, but I kind of liked being in that old building. It was as quiet as a library, a cool dark retreat from the furnace that was Arkansas in June. Polished oak banisters slid easily under my hand, and the ancient stairs creaked under my weight. Lithographs of Berryville as it had been fifty years ago dotted the walls of the stairwell. Back then, there was no fountain in the town square, just a massive concrete bandstand with lead pipe railing all around. Hitching posts stood around the edge of the square like tiny soldiers.

One of the faded pictures showed the Berryville Mercantile, which still occupies nearly a half block on the northeastern side of the square. The awning sagged less then, and the clothes on the mannequins had changed with the times.

Another lithograph showed an open-air blacksmith shop filled with old, self-conscious looking men who stared right into the camera. A Chevy dealership occupies the old blacksmith's shed now, which is kind of an appropriate exchange—mechanical horsepower for the four-footed kind.

One lithograph stood out from the rest. It was of a small shop, the only building occupying space at the junction of two of the streets enclosing the town square. Twin barber poles flanked the doors opened wide in welcome. A smiling young man in his early twenties stood directly in front of one of the poles, so it appeared to be growing from the top of his head. The man in the picture was really decked out. I think "dapper" is the word they would have used to describe him in the 1920s. His clothes looked crisp and new and probably expensive.

"That suit cost me a month's salary," said a voice behind me. "But, by God, I was a dandy." The speaker chuckled to himself and then to me as I turned to face him.

"You mean that's you in the picture?" I must have sounded more surprised than I intended. The man behind me was short, about five-foot four, but he looked even smaller because his shoulders were rounded and stooped. He held his hands clasped behind his back so his elbows stuck out at his sides.

"Yep, taken when I first started clipping hair in Berryville. I went all the way to Springfield for that suit." The old guy's love for stylish clothes must have faded over the years. He wore baggy brown slacks supported by narrow suspenders, an over-starched white shirt, and a western-style string tie fastened with an unpolished agate clasp. Heavily framed bifocals bridged his nose, and his ears stuck out slightly. He was nearly bald. What little hair he had was light enough to be barely noticeable.

I didn't know whether or not to take this guy seriously. "Do you still barber around here?" I asked.

"I do indeed," he answered. "Same place, too. If you want to see more, come on up to the third floor. They've got a few things from my early days at the shop up there," he noted with pride.

He was referring to the Pioneer Heritage Center Museum on the top floor of the courthouse. I had been up there a couple of times with a class from The Cedars, but I had never seen anything like the old guy was describing.

"Howdy, Mr. Skipworth," Sheriff Stoner stepped in. "Sorry, sir, but Benedict—this one here, Ross Benedict—is in my custody. The damn fool just dyed the fountain with red ink or something. The red's got into the limestone, too. I'm guessing the whole thing will need to be drained and the pump cleaned before we're through."

"That right, boy?" Mr. Skipworth seemed concerned.

"What's it to you, old timer?" I grunted with a sarcasm I didn't feel. I stuck my stained hands in my pockets. "Let's go, Sheriff."

As we walked into Stoner's office, I turned for one last glimpse of Mr. Skipworth. He was still standing in front of that lithograph of himself, but he was looking at me.

Three

A Proposition

Sheriff Stoner lost no time processing the necessary paper work. He asked me about a thousand questions and scowled when he didn't like my answers, which was most of the time. Finally, he looked up at me with a grin of satisfaction.

"Well, Benedict, I've been waiting for you to slip up, and now you've obliged me. With your track record, I'll have no trouble getting you a reservation at the reformatory. Until we can schedule a hearing, though, I'll treat you to a little of my hospitality."

It was finally beginning to sink in. This wasn't like all the other times. I'd pushed Stoner too far, and there wasn't a soul in the world who gave a damn. Even in that June heat, I could feel my hands turn clammy. I couldn't keep my show of indifference up much longer, not with Stoner's mocking face in front of me.

With a final show of contempt, I curled my lip in a sneer before I lowered my head.

"Excuse me, Sheriff, but a young man from the county attorney's office is here," interrupted Stoner's secretary. "He says he has to see you. Now."

Terrific, I thought. These guys are so anxious to throw me to the lions, they can't even wait for Stoner to send the reports to them.

Stoner looked like he was holding a royal flush in a high stakes poker game. "Stay put," he commanded as he left the room.

I strained to hear the muffled exchange between Stoner and the newcomer, but I couldn't catch more than a couple of words. Once, the sheriff roared, "Not a chance in hell." The other guy hushed him up right away, and I didn't hear anything else.

Eventually Stoner clumped back into the office. He was followed by a younger man who carried a small briefcase.

With barely controlled restraint, Stoner said, "I'll be damned if I know why, but it looks like your neck's off the block—at least for now. That old guy you were so *kind* to," he said sarcastically, "has decided to pull your ass out of the fire if you meet his conditions." Some of the tension must have drained from my face, because Stoner added, "You're a fool kid who has another chance. Don't screw this one up."

"I'm Mr. Phelps, Ross," Sheriff Stoner's

companion interjected. "I'm with the county attorney's office. A few minutes ago, I had a visit from Mr. Skipworth. I believe the two of you know each other. He has asked I make his wishes known."

Phelps continued, "The terms of the proposition are simple enough. Mr. Skipworth has agreed to pay for any costs associated with cleaning and repairing the fountain. In turn, you work off the debt at his barber shop."

"Who is this guy?" I asked. "What's his deal?"

Phelps kept talking as if he hadn't heard me. "Additionally, since we don't have juvenile facilities in Berryville, he'll put you up—I'm talking room and board here—at his place. He doesn't seem to think the school's been a very good influence on you, apparently. All charges against you will be dropped if you keep your nose clean."

"Who *is* this guy?" I repeated. "How come he gets to call the shots?"

"Mr. Skipworth has somewhat of a reputation around these parts, son. You're not the first kid who's ever messed up. Let's leave it at that. All you need to know is the county is willing to go along with the deal as long as everyone agrees to the terms."

"So, what's it gonna be?" Stoner asked.

Were these guys kidding? Choosing between a rap sheet and reformatory school or doing two-bit chores for some old man was like being offered rancid fish or the Colonel's Kentucky Fried. This was laughable, it really was.

"I'll take the offer. And I'll try to make it right with the old guy," I lied. I was already thinking how easy it would be to con this geezer into just about anything.

"Well, then, it's settled," Phelps said. "You're to begin at once, Ross. I'll escort you to Mr. Skipworth's shop. Don't worry about your things. The sheriff can make a trip to the school. Just let me get my hat."

This was too easy. I couldn't resist a parting shot to Stoner, though. "Oh, by the way, while you're at The Cedars, would you sorta straighten out my room? I hate leaving a bad impression."

So, for the second time that day, I headed across the town square in the company of a city official. This time, the walk was far from silent. Phelps obviously liked to talk, and I was pumping him for all the information about Mr. Skipworth I could get.

Evidently, the old guy was pretty well known around town. As Berryville's oldest barber, he had been around over half a century. According to Phelps, Mr. Skipworth was a self-made man, widely read, who was generally respected and admired. The fact he never attended any of Berryville's many churches was his one major flaw in the eyes of this Bible-belt community. Most of his customers were on the far side of fifty, but he had a steady stream of friends and acquaintances who dropped in just to pass the time. He lived alone on a farm four miles south of town. Before his wife Faye had died some twenty years earlier, she had worked in a beauty shop housed in the same building where Mr. Skipworth barbered. He had never remarried.

Sketchy as that background was, I still figured I had the upper hand. Mr. Skipworth knew next to nothing about me, and I planned on keeping it that way. With a smile any choir boy would have been proud of, I led the way through the double doors into Mr. Skipworth's shop.

Four

The Barber of Berryville

In spite of myself, I couldn't help the surprise that must have registered on my face when I first stepped into the room. I had intended to give Mr. Skipworth a lot of crap about how generous I thought his offer was, but when Phelps and I entered the barber shop, I seemed to lose all sense of myself. It was as though I had time-traveled back into the last century. Every stick of furniture, every fixture, every picture looked like props from some old silent movie.

Since the double doorway was located at one of the building's corners, the rest of the room was laid out like a baseball diamond is to home plate. I went down the "first base line," a mostly glass wall. There was an elevated window well packed with all kinds of rocks and fossils and samples of petrified wood. Open textbooks were scattered among the specimens, and each page was somehow related to the rock sample beside it. In one of the books, I could see an artist's drawing of a bunch of toothy fish swimming around a cone-shaped creature. The caption identified a cephalopod. Sure enough, the fossil next to the book was a cephalopod's broken tail. Other specimens were also classified and labeled. Sunlight, filtered through dusty bottles of rainbow-colored hair tonic, painted the whole collection.

There were lots of things besides rocks and fossils, though, like games and arrowhead collections mounted on display boards and puzzles I'd never seen before. One of the coolest things was a tiny man made entirely from carpenters' nails—the old, square-headed kind. He looked like one of those stick figures you draw when you play Hangman, and he held a crescent-shaped balancing pole which curved down below his feet. Standing on top of a bottle of hair tonic, the toy man would swing back and forth with each slight breeze, but he never fell from his perch.

The work area occupied space between "first" and "second" in the barbershop diamond. Three barber chairs, their white porcelain bases solidly planted in the floor, dominated the room. They were mostly made of scrolled metal, and they resembled huge mushrooms with oval backs and enamel arm rests. Deep, wine-colored leather upholstery, attached to the frames with dull brass brads, covered the puffy seats and chair backs. Worn leather razor strops hung almost to the floor from each of the chairs.

Mr. Skipworth was sitting in the chair closest to the window well. He was reading the *Berryville Star Progress*. I couldn't see his face, but the back of his head was reflected in the mirror which ran the length of the room. Beneath the mirror and an arm's length behind each chair were old porcelain sinks with exposed plumbing. Several shelves stocked with assorted razors, scissors, combs, and lather mugs flanked each of the sinks.

An old wood burning stove, now converted to a gas heater, and a Kiwanis gumball machine were the only items reflected in the mirror that continued around the corner and down toward "third base." The home stretch was filled with a coat tree, uncomfortable-looking benches for waiting customers, and a dilapidated shoeshine stand littered with tins of shoe wax, brushes, and polishing cloths. Over our heads, an antique wooden ceiling fan whirred. The annoying drone was a small price to pay for the cool relief from the early summer heat.

As soon as Mr. Skipworth made sure I had seen everything, he methodically folded his paper and walked slowly toward Phelps and me.

"That didn't take long," he said. "I'm glad you've decided to come work for me, young man. You can start by cleaning up the shine stand. Then I'll show you the rest of the operation."

"Thank you for your help, Mr. Phelps," he continued. "And good day." For an old guy, Mr. Skipworth knew how to get rid of Phelps politely without beating around the bush.

Phelps looked as if he expected to help me adjust to this new situation, but he shrugged his shoulders, nodded to me, and said to Mr. Skipworth, "I'll be in touch about the boy's progress."

I was finally alone with Mr. Skipworth. "I want you to know, sir, how much I appreciate what you're doing. I mean, nobody's ever…"

"Don't insult me, son," Mr. Skipworth interrupted. "We both know you didn't have any other choice but reform school. This is probably the next to the last place you want to be, but maybe, if you talk plain and say what you mean, we can both come out winners."

"Hey, man," I broke in defensively. "I'm not trying to con you. I just wanted to…"

"What you wanted to do," interjected Mr. Skipworth, "was bowl me over with a lot of meaningless talk. You'll do well to remember I judge a man by what he is and what he does, not by what he says he's going to do." I knew how Phelps must have felt when Mr. Skipworth dismissed him so efficiently. There was absolutely nothing left for me to say.

Okay, then, I vowed to myself. *You get the silent treatment, old man.*

Five

Down Payment on a Debt

I was hard pressed to keep my oath of silence that afternoon. Mr. Skipworth didn't seem to notice, much less care about getting the cold shoulder. In fact, when he talked, it was almost like he was talking to himself rather than telling me what I was supposed to do.

The shoeshine stand was my first test. Mr. Skipworth pointed out the tins of waxes and saddle soaps. He told me which kinds of wax to use on different types of boots and showed me how to produce a shine that would satisfy even Marines in boot camp. I began practicing on Mr. Skipworth's wingtips, but I couldn't make the polishing cloth snap against the leather the way he did. My frustration must have shown, because he said I shouldn't expect too much in the first few tries.

"Leave that. You'll get plenty of chances to

practice. Why don't you get all those dirty towels and bring them to the back room." He led the way through a narrow curtained door next to the gas heater. If I had paid attention to my gut, I would have slithered out the front door and taken my chances with Stoner. Instead, I piled the towels in my arms and followed Warden Skipworth.

The room I entered was as dark and shadowy as the shop was bright. The only light came from a small window high above my head. Once my eyes adjusted to the dimness, I could make out a huge roll top desk just inside the door. The desk was almost hidden under the clutter of paper and envelopes, bills, books, and assorted rusty hardware. Beyond the desk hung several rows of clotheslines sagging under the weight of freshly laundered towels. Scraps of lumber and sheetrock leaned against the wall.

Mr. Skipworth led me to an old, footed bathtub. "I've always hated doing towels in that tub," he complained.

Imagining Mr. Skipworth struggling over the tub with sopping towels made me smile, at least for a minute.

"That'll be another job for you." He paused, remembering. "Used to be that bathtub saw different action. Years ago, families from outlying farms came to town. Women would do the marketing and visit while the men did their bank business and stopped to post mail or check on an order at the feed store. Then they'd come here for a shave, haircut, and a bath. I used to keep the shop open late every Saturday—'til nine or ten, maybe, but things have changed over the years. Anyway, I always meant to have a different set-up for washing these towels. I just never got around to it. I'm glad you'll be taking care of that now."

I'll bet you are, I thought, as I pitched the towels in the tub and began filling it with water and detergent.

The slam of the double screen doors announced the arrival of a customer. Mr. Skipworth disappeared into the shop.

"Howdy," I heard him say. "No waiting this afternoon." I heard the shuffle of feet as Mr. Skipworth directed the man to a chair. I ventured a peek through the curtains. Mr. Skipworth had put on a dorky visor with a green plastic bill and was wrapping a narrow strip of tissue around his customer's neck. This was followed by a huge sheet-like apron which covered the man from his neck to his knees. Mr. Skipworth pumped the chair up to a comfortable height and began mixing a foamy concoction in one of the ceramic mugs. With a short brush, he expertly lathered the man's face and neck. He stropped a tortoise shell handled razor with rapid strokes and began to scrape away at the man's beard.

Just then, I heard a waterfall gushing behind me. I had forgotten the tub, filling with sudsy water, and was now helplessly watching the overflow that resembled the runoff at Beaver Dam. Making a mad dash toward the tub, I turned off the faucets and looked at the pool of standing water. Hoping Mr. Skipworth would be busy with his customer for awhile, I hunted frantically for a mop and bucket.

My search led me to a small room beyond the curtains surrounding the tub. A single, bare bulb revealed a scarred refrigerator with an old screwdriver jimmied into the handle. Next to the refrigerator stood a card table which held a greasy hot plate and a couple of battered aluminum sauce pans. I imagined Mr. Skipworth all alone eating lunch in that miserable cubbyhole, day in and day out, and I felt just a little bit sorry for him. Not much, but a little.

I found the mop and bucket and slowly returned to the flood on the floor. Because I could still hear Mr. Skipworth's scissors snipping along, I figured I had plenty of time to get rid of the evidence. I was just squeezing the last of the water into the bucket when I heard the bells on the cash register ring, followed by the slam of the screen doors.

"So, you found the mop, eh?" Mr. Skipworth observed from the door. "I've had that same thing happen a lot of times. Usually, I don't find out about it 'til the water starts creeping under the curtain into the shop. One time," he laughed," I was with a customer when it happened. I left him, half lathered up, sitting in the chair. When I finally got back to him, he had fallen sound asleep. He was so limp, I thought for a minute he was dead, but then he started snoring. I just didn't have the heart to wake him up, so he slept most of the afternoon. When he woke up, the lather was so caked his face looked like a dried up river bed in the middle of a drought. He never came back for a shave or cut, but he stops in now and again just to talk."

I had been trying to think of some excuse to explain my screw-up with the tub, but with his simple story, Mr. Skipworth had saved me from manufacturing a lie to save face. He also spared me from breaking my self-inflicted silence, which—if you want to know the truth—was getting a little tiresome by then.

Although I stayed stubbornly silent for the rest of the afternoon, much of my earlier resentment for Mr. Skipworth was melting away. He had a comment or funny recollection about almost every customer, and so I really had a tough time remembering not to talk to him. Still, he made no mention of my silence, and the minutes ticked away. By the five o'clock closing time, I had shined three pairs of shoes, washed who knows how many towels, and cleaned the entire sixty-foot expanse of mirror.

In fact, I had been so busy, I hadn't thought about anything beyond the work. When the last customer had critically surveyed his appearance in the mirror, paid for his haircut and left, I realized I wasn't going back to Loser Central. Mr. Skipworth hadn't said anything about dinner or where I was going to bunk. I figured it was his way of getting me to talk, but I was wrong again.

"As soon as we sweep up," said Mr. Skipworth, "we'll go on out to the house for some supper. Here, take this." He handed me a broom from the back room. I started to sweep around the base of the barber chairs, but Mr. Skipworth told me to wait until he got the sawdust. If I had been talking to him, I would have asked him what in the name of Judas he meant, but he seemed to answer my questions almost before I even thought of them.

"I use this oiled sawdust," he explained as he tossed handful after handful of the tacky stuff on the floor. "If I don't, this hair flies all over everything. It's like raking leaves in a hurricane."

I swept up the sawdust along with the day's accumulation of hair and dumped the whole mess into a gigantic cardboard box which was already nearly full. The sawdust had done the trick, and it also accounted for the dark luster of the wooden floor.

"That's a good job done," observed Mr. Skipworth as he removed a long pole hanging from the coat tree. With a quick flick of his wrist, Mr. Skipworth used the notched end to switch off the motor at the ceiling fan's base. The momentum of the rotating blades kept the fan in motion for a few seconds before it whirred to a stop. The silence was immense and so was the heat.

At the door, Mr. Skipworth waited for me. "Let's go home, Ross."

Six

Room and Board

Without meaning to, Mr. Skipworth forced me to speak that afternoon. No, check that. I should say he forced me to scream from sheer terror. Believe me, the Salem Witch Trials were child's play compared to a single automobile ride with Mr. Skipworth at the wheel.

The nightmare began when I climbed into Mr. Skipworth's car, a white '64 Chevy Impala in mint condition with only twenty-nine thousand miles. Mr. Skipworth said he only drove to and from work, a round trip of eight miles. There wasn't a single paint chip or a speck of rust anywhere on the body. The interior was almost new, too. Plastic sheets still covered the back seats, and there was only a little wear on the upholstery in the front.

Surprisingly, the engine sputtered and coughed as

Mr. Skipworth revved the motor. I guessed even in eleven years the car hadn't seen enough hard driving to really blow out the kinks. We moved slowly through the one-way streets around the town square. Once on the highway leading south, however, he nudged the Chevy up to about sixty and began playing the role of a tour guide on a sight-seeing bus. He would point out the landmark he was describing, but because he kept his hand on the wheel as he pointed, the car swerved from side to side with each gesture. Sometimes two wheels were completely off the highway before Mr. Skipworth guided the car back under control. Even through all that, I kept a white-knuckled grip on the dash without screaming. I finally surrendered, though, as we neared a one-lane bridge spanning the Osage River. If Mr. Skipworth misjudged our approach, we'd slam into the concrete restraining rails or—worse yet—plunge into the river. There wasn't much chance of drowning. The mighty Osage is only a mere trickle, but I didn't relish the idea of going swimming dressed in a '64 Chevy Impala.

"For Chrissakes, look out!" I screamed to Mr. Skipworth, who was pointing at—and heading for—a stand of trees covered with bagworms. Just in time, he corrected our course and we sped across the bridge.

"What's that?" asked Mr. Skipworth, as though he hadn't just scared me spitless. Little did Sheriff Stoner know when he placed me in the protective custody of one Mr. Luther Skipworth, he very nearly killed me.

Thankful I had managed not to piss myself, I could only murmur a sickly, "Nothing."

Relatively speaking, the rest of the ride was uneventful. We still occasionally veered toward Arnell Jesup's herd of buffalo or the Blue Mountain Chain Saw Company or Farmer's Cemetery, but I took that all in stride. Five minutes later we rounded the corner at the peak of a small incline. The valley below us nestled in a patchwork of sunlight and shadow. Mr. Skipworth told me his land began at the hill's summit and extended down both sides of the highway until the next bend in the road, about 190 acres altogether. Because the rocky earth wasn't good for crops, Mr. Skipworth raised cattle. Several of his Whiteface Herefords lazily grazed on the scrubby hillside or lolled in the shade of towering cedar trees. The Chevy's tires bit into Mr. Skipworth's gravel driveway. We were home.

"Here we are, Ross. How does it look?"

Because of my recent brush with death, anything that didn't move looked terrific. The house wasn't really that special—just a white stucco rectangle situated on an overgrown lawn. A black metal "S" decorated a whitewashed board hanging from the gutter. Huge, thick shrubs hid the foundation of the house. Against the garage leaned two slabs of rock, their surfaces etched with lacy fossils.

Only when Mr. Skipworth eased the Chevy into the attached garage and turned off the engine did my heart stop racing. With rubber arms I opened the car door, but almost instantly slammed it shut and frantically fumbled to close the window. An immense head and two gigantic forefeet belonging to a snarling German shepherd shot toward me through the open window.

"Geraldine. Down, girl!" ordered Mr. Skipworth. The dog obediently dropped to all fours and sat eyeing me. She was probably waiting for the *kill* command. "Here now, come on. It's all right, Ross. She's just overly friendly."

"You're sure she won't bite?" I ventured, peering over the rim of the car window.

"No, she's just anxious to say hello. Easy, Geraldine. Easy, girl."

Once Geraldine knew I was on Mr. Skipworth's list of approved guests, she wagged her tail in friendly greeting. Still, I stepped cautiously from the car and edged my way toward the door like a suicide case would move on the ledge of a building. The dog anointed my hand with a slobbery swipe of her tongue and gently nudged me on my way.

It was no small accomplishment to have made it into the kitchen. I stood silently for a moment before I began to look around at my new digs. Although Mr. Skipworth didn't go in for twentieth century conveniences in his shop, I was grateful he allowed a few of them inside the house. A hot water heater was clanking away just inside the door, and I could see a big chest freezer and a washing machine on the enclosed sleeping porch just beyond the next room. Otherwise, he probably would have had me beating his laundry on rocks down at the Osage.

I was anxious to see the rest of the place, but my stomach always overrules my curiosity. I was really hungry. The chips and Dr. Pepper at the Berryville Drug hadn't stayed with me long. It seemed like days since I had eaten.

"What's for supper?"

"You can have your choice, Ross. Usually I don't eat much, but I'm a bit hungry myself tonight," Mr. Skipworth admitted. "I can scramble some eggs for us, and there's a few leftover doughnuts from the bakery," he offered. "Or if you want, I think there's some biscuits in the refrigerator."

Without hesitating, I answered, "Let's have both." I opened the refrigerator in search of biscuits. I didn't have to look far. On the door's lower shelf, where most people keep mayonnaise and pickles and Italian dressing, were about twenty tubes of refrigerated biscuits. Shooting a furtive glance at Mr. Skipworth, I pulled one of the tubes from its place and set it on the counter.

"Better open a couple, Ross," Mr. Skipworth

instructed. "I could make a meal out of hot bread."

As I prepared the biscuits, Mr. Skipworth disappeared through a door at the rear of the kitchen. While he changed, he whistled, and when he came back, he was dressed in a short-sleeve cotton work suit and old leather cowboy boots.

"Let's get to it," he commanded. Taking a half dozen eggs from the refrigerator, he cracked the shells, dropped their contents into a bowl and whisked them together with some evaporated milk and a little salt and pepper. From the oven he pulled a well-greased iron skillet and set it on the front burner. He lit the pilot with one hand and with the other scooped up a heaping tablespoon of bacon drippings from a canister on the counter. When the grease was sizzling in the pan, Mr. Skipworth dumped in the foamy yellow eggs and turned to me.

"Butter's in the fridge and the sorghum's on the shelf in the pantry. Plates are in the cupboard left of the refrigerator, and the silverware is in the top drawer." Mr. Skipworth pulled out a built-in bread board and told me to pull up two kitchen stools. "We'll eat here, Ross. Just put everything down here." He went back to his eggs, which were just beginning to puff at the edges.

I found the dishes and silverware and set them on the breadboard.

"Don't forget the sorghum," reminded Mr.

Skipworth, gesturing with his elbow toward the pantry.

Judging by the contents of the pantry, you would have thought a family of twelve lived in the farmhouse instead of just one old man. Cases of canned goods, mostly vegetables like corn and peas and beans, shared the shelf space with fruits, several boxes of cereal (all the sugar-coated type), and jar after jar of jams and jellies and fruit butters. Enormous plastic bins on the floor held mounds of sweet red onions and large, firm potatoes. If nothing else, I thought, I'm going to eat well.

"Come on, Ross. These biscuits are done and the eggs will get cold."

I grabbed one of the jars of sorghum and perched myself on a stool at the breadboard. Mr. Skipworth divided the eggs between us and placed the first pan of bread on the counter.

I burned my fingers trying to scoop out the first flaky biscuit, but that didn't stop me for a second. Before the butter had time to melt into a yellow pool, I had stuffed the whole biscuit into my mouth. Good thing Mr. Skipworth had insisted I make a double batch of bread.

The eggs and biscuits hadn't taken much time or effort, but I can't remember a better meal. Mr. Skipworth must have liked the food as much as I did, because he barely spoke throughout supper. With him, eating was a business. He wolfed down the eggs in six or seven bites and polished off biscuits like it was his job. If the *Guinness Book of World Records* had a "Champion Biscuit Eater of All Time" category, Mr. Skipworth would be a shoo-in. By actual count, he downed thirteen biscuits in about twenty minutes. The best part is the *way* he took them down. He called it "making soppy." He started with about three big pats of butter drowned in a river of sorghum. He mashed the mess together, forked a biscuit, tore it in half, and used it as a sponge to "sop" up the gooey mixture.

His eating didn't gross me out, though, no matter how bad it sounds. Mr. Skipworth just enjoyed his meal, and he didn't care who knew it. I got the feeling, once or twice, he hadn't always gotten to eat as much as he wanted as often as he wanted. Maybe that explained his appetite and the hoard in the pantry.

Suddenly, in the middle of the fourteenth biscuit, Mr. Skipworth stopped eating. "I believe I've had sufficient," he announced. He pushed his plate an inch or so away from him and rested his elbows on the table. He belched—deep, rolling, and long—and sighed in satisfaction.

"I could make a meal on hot bread," he said. "Yep, I'd just as soon have that as anything else."

In my future days with Mr. Skipworth, I learned he could actually "make a meal" on cornbread and beans or fried meat and potatoes or baked chicken or cobbler or... Well, you get the idea.

"If you'll excuse me, I believe I'll take a look at the news," he said. Mr. Skipworth rose and headed for the sink. Without ceremony, he pulled out his upper and lower dentures and rinsed them under running water. They clicked together as he replaced them, juggling them with his tongue. When he couldn't seem to get them in the right position, he casually dropped them into a glass of water on the counter. I made an immediate mental note: *NEVER, EVER, under any circumstances, drink from* that *glass.* He shuffled past me toward what I guessed must be the living room without so much as a backward glance at me. It was just me and the dirty dishes.

We'll have to see about this, I thought. Just because I had a debt to pay for the business in town didn't make me a kitchen slave on the farm.

As it was, though, cleaning up didn't even take a half an hour, and I had some time to think about how fast things can change. I hung up the wet dishtowel, smiled to myself, and followed the voice of the TV announcer through the darkened dining area and on into the living room.

Seven

Required Reading

Mr. Skipworth was straining to hear the weather forecast for Sunday. He was stretched out in a recliner, his hands clasped behind his head and his eyes squinted in concentration. I plopped down on one of the two big couches and listened as the weatherman predicted another humid day, not exactly earth shattering news. When the anchorman had recapped the day's headlines, Mr. Skipworth flipped off the set and gave me his full attention.

"Do you read much, Ross?"

Here it comes, I thought. "Well, in school...," I began.

"Everybody should read. That's the way you learn things. That's the way you find out about this old world." He stood up and shuffled over to stand behind the couch where I was sitting. "I've got some books here everybody should read. These books make you think."

He waved his hand toward a bookcase that filled the wall behind me. Books were wedged so tightly into the case Mr. Skipworth had difficulty pulling his favorite selections from the shelves. All the books were nonfiction, and most of the titles dealt with nature, wildlife, geology, or ancient history. Rows of brilliant yellow bindings stretched across the bottom two shelves, and I noticed Mr. Skipworth's collection of *National Geographic* dated back to 1954.

"...and this one shows X-ray photos of ancient Egyptian kings," Mr. Skipworth was saying. He pointed to a grisly picture of some pharaoh's mummified body, photographed right through his linen wrappings.

"Now these," he continued as he piled book after book next to me on the sofa, "these books tell me everything I want to know. They tell me the truth about this world, the truth as I see it. Take a look, boy."

I began flipping through a book on the geological history of the world he'd given me, looking at pictures, reading captions, and skimming paragraphs. Apparently satisfied, Mr. Skipworth returned to his chair, picked up the Springfield paper, and began reading.

I must have read longer than I thought. When I

looked up, it was almost nine o'clock. Mr. Skipworth's head was thrown back, his mouth wide open. At first, I thought he must be laughing, but without any sound. Instead, he was dead to the world.

Without disturbing him, I got up and stretched. I rubbed my eyes and went in search of the bathroom. A cool shower sounded good.

The bathroom was in bad shape. Hard water rust stains ringed the sink's drain and the toilet was squat and chipped. I found a towel that had seen better days hanging from a rack outside the shower stall. Wondering what I was going to do for a change of clothes, I peeled off my jeans and shirt and underwear and kicked them in a pile. Geraldine was barking furiously as I stepped into the shower, and I heard Mr. Skipworth call my name.

"In the shower," I yelled. "I hope that's okay." When I didn't hear him answer, I stepped into the shower and turned on the faucets full blast. Needlelike jets of water stung me for all of about five seconds, then the pressure dropped and water sputtered and spit until it was a miserable little trickle. The temperature did a number on me too, scalding one minute and icy the next.

"Damn," I muttered as I fumbled for the faucets. In the end, I lathered up and rinsed off as best I could.

I cringed as I put my dirty Levis back on, hoping I could ditch them for something from Mr. Skipworth's closet. Surely he'd have something that would fit. I walked back into the living room, surprised to see my large canvas duffel bag sitting by the hearth. Evidently Sheriff Stoner had dropped off my things from The Cedars while I'd been showering.

Stoner hadn't exactly treated my things with tender loving care. My clothes had been stuffed into the bag along with my sneakers and hiking boots. My comb and toothbrush and shampoo were thrown in as well.

"Where should I put this, Mr. Skipworth?"

"You can have your choice of the middle bedroom or the one at the end of the hall."

Choosing was no contest. The bedroom at the end of the hall had the advantage of being the furthest from Mr. Skipworth's room, prime real estate for someone who has made his share of undetected late night exits from more than one foster home. The location didn't begin to offset the museum-like feel of the place, though. Framed pictures lined the walls, but no Kodak Brownie snapshots of picnics or birthday parties or camping trips for Mr. Skipworth's guest bedroom. Nope. All of them were formal studio portraits finished in that brown tone that made the subjects look like they'd been dipped in bronze plastic. The largest display, a triple set of eight by tens, hung on the wall opposite the double bed, and it was easy to identify a younger Mr. Skipworth in the frame on the left. He had more hair—not longer, just darker—and fewer wrinkles, but the grin was the same. On the right was a pretty, dark-haired woman I guessed must have been his wife. Although her grin wasn't nearly as broad as Mr. Skipworth's, her expression almost made me feel like she was sharing a private joke with herself. I found myself thinking she must have been fun to be around. Whether by accident or intent, the two faces in the portraits were angled toward the center, as though they were smiling at the image of the young woman captured there in three-quarter profile. The picture was a full-length shot, and the girl wore a dress of white lace. She, too, had thick, dark hair, and I guessed she probably had the guys panting for her in school. I wondered why Mr. S stuck these pictures in a room that, judging by the dust on the furniture, he probably never entered. If I'd had such a good-looking family, I'd probably plaster their pictures on a billboard on the highway.

I checked out the middle bedroom and instantly claimed it as mine. Even though the furniture was a little girly—an antique bed with matching mirrored dressing table (maybe once used by the girl in the white dress?)—I knew I'd be bunking here because that's where Mr. Skipworth kept his glass-front cedar gun case. His collection included a Remington, its stock all polished and gleaming. He also had a .22 pistol in a real leather gun belt. I laughed to think of

Stoner's reaction if he knew I had such an arsenal at my disposal.

Changing into a semi-clean pair of jeans and a short-sleeved shirt, I walked back into the living room to find Mr. Skipworth warming up the set for the ten o'clock news. I wasn't too hyped about a repeat performance of the news, but I didn't know what else to do. I thought about going outside for a look around, but I wasn't used to the inkiness of a country night. At The Cedars, mercury vapor lamps lit the grounds around the dorm and rec hall all night. Sunday would be soon enough for a closer inspection of the farm. Taking my position on the couch, I watched the last few minutes of a gangster flick with Mr. Skipworth.

The news was the same as at six o'clock. I began to yawn from sheer boredom. Mr. Skipworth was doing the same from sheer exhaustion. Promptly at 10:30, he rose and headed for his room.

"I'll leave it with you, Ross. Good night."

There was no way I was going to follow his lead. At The Cedars, if anyone tried to hit the sack before midnight, he would have been short-sheeted or pennied into his room. In fact, I remembered the night K.D. and Major had done just that. I was finishing a homework assignment that, for once, would be on time, when I heard *BLAM, BLAM, BLAM* just outside my door. We had metal doors at The Cedars because of fire regulations, and the pounding echoed throughout the dorm. Then I heard Major howling his head off. He and K.D. had wedged pennies between my closed door and the doorjamb and pounded them in with a big rubber mallet. It was like locking me in my room from the outside. Then they poured dirty mop water under the crack at the bottom of my door. Not even the maintenance guy could get me out, so they had to call the fire department to break down the door. The head man at The Cedars blew a gasket when he found out. The three of us had to split the cost of replacing the door in addition to working clean-up duty in the toilets for six weeks. That first night at the farm, I was really missing the excitement from those stunts we pulled at The Cedars, believe me.

Sitting alone in the living room, I was wide-eyed and bored as hell. I didn't want to read anymore, at least not from the books Mr. Skipworth had given me. Wandering around the room, I tried to find something to keep me from climbing the walls. Unexpectedly, I found what I was looking for.

Under the end table beside Mr. Skipworth's recliner was a battered leather scrapbook, its pages worn from constant thumbing through. Some of the newspaper clippings had escaped from beneath brittle pieces of old Scotch tape and were ragged and wrinkled as a result. Most of the articles had come from the Springfield paper, and some dated as far back as 1946. They covered topics on Mr. Skipworth's pet interests—history, archaeology, natural science—but there were also stories about freaks of nature and unexplained events. I found a news story about a geological dig where archaeologists discovered evidence of human sacrifice predating the Roman Conquest in Carthage. There was an eyewitness account of a girl who had escaped a religious cult and an editorial that screamed "Venereal Disease Increasing; Rise Among Youth Shocking."

Between some of the pages I found dozens of little scraps of paper scrawled with odd, short statements:

The world is my country and to do good is my religion.

People with one track minds often have derailed trains of thought.

It is not whether there is life after death, but whether life is worth living after birth.

At the banquet table of life, each in turn is a guest and a dish.

Each little epigram was signed with Mr. Skipworth's given name, "Luther," although I was pretty sure he wasn't the author. The statements sounded more like something out of the "Quotable Quotes" section of *Reader's Digest*.

I found only two entries which directly involved Mr. Skipworth. The first was an obituary from the *Berryville Star Progress* for a Mr. William "Old Bill" Dimmick. Old Bill had lived and worked on the farm with Mr. Skipworth for a long time. A dark, poorly reproduced photo showed Old Bill hard at work, but his features were hidden by a shapeless, floppy hat. Old Bill had died when he was eighty-three and had been buried beside Faye, the late Mrs. Luther Skipworth, in the cemetery south of Berryville. I figured the cemetery must be the same one we passed on the way home from the shop. Out of curiosity, I promised myself to visit the graves of the two people closest to Mr. Skipworth as soon as I had the chance.

The second newspaper clipping caught my eye with its bold headline: "Mrs. Sam Skipworth Accidently Killed." I barely passed freshman English at The Cedars, but I still knew "accidently" was misspelled. The rest of the article was a total mess, and I wondered if the style of writing was typical of small town news stories from hick papers in the early 1900s. I knew for certain my teacher would have written "Awkward!" and "Run-on sentence!" and "Did you proofread?????" all over the margins of the obituary.

ALTON, MISSOURI
October 17, 1910
   MRS. SAM SKIPWORTH ACCIDENTLY KILLED When Wagon Wheel Strikes Stump and Spring Seat Breaks, Throwing Her In Front of the Wagon

On last Monday evening Mr. and Mrs. Sam Skipworth, living three miles north of Many Springs, had been out to Greer's Mill and had started back home rather late. Mr. Skipworth was driving at a pretty rapid rate, in order to get home before dark, and had gotten almost home, when the front wheel of the wagon came in contact with a small stump at the side of the road, causing the spring seat to break and pitching Mrs. Skipworth, who held a small baby in her arms in front of the wagon, both front and hind wheel passing over her breast in an instant almost crushing the life from her, but the baby was practically uninjured. Dr. Piles was summoned to the scene and went as quick as he could and got there just a few minutes before life left her. She was the daughter of Mr. Dave Teague and leaves a husband, six children and a host of other relatives and friends.

When I realized the lady who died must have been Mr. Skipworth's mother, I felt like I'd been gut punched. Mr. Skipworth might be an old codger now, but he had been a little kid once, and he had seen his mom die in a horrible accident. I spent my whole life feeling sorry for myself because I never had a mom who cared about me. Did Mr. Skipworth have it worse? He'd at least known his mom, known she'd loved him, and then she was gone. Did he feel cheated too?

I found out much later Mr. Skipworth had one brother and four sisters, and soon after his mom died the kids were separated. His family saw a need to keep the girls together, but the boys were split up and shuffled from one relative to another. The sisters were brought up by a strict, religious aunt. Mr. Skipworth grew up more like me—fighting every step of the way. He said he didn't have much faith in God because, as far as he could tell, God hadn't done him any favors. His anger made for some bitter arguments between Mr. Skipworth and his sisters later in life.

Don't get me wrong. Mr. Skipworth would never have told me any of this, no matter what. I was able to make some guesses on my own, based on some overheard conversations and snatches of letters Mr. Skipworth would occasionally read to me. His daughter, Jorita, filled in most of the gaps when she and her family visited in August, but that's a story in itself, and I'll deal with it later.

All I can remember, sitting silently holding that scrapbook in the empty living room, is the comfort I felt because I knew I wasn't alone.

Eight

Beauty, Babe, and a Little Bull

Sunday morning started earlier than usual for me. The eastern sun blazed in through the living room window, making me feel like an actor on a stage. I had fallen asleep in Mr. Skipworth's recliner, the opened scrapbook still on my lap. I returned the album to its place on the floor, stood up, and stretched. Every joint was stiff. Every muscle ached. I decided to walk around outside and work off some of the tightness. Grabbing a shirt only slightly less wrinkled than the one I was wearing, I slipped through the kitchen door into the garage and edged around the Chevy.

A steep flight of concrete steps led to a sundeck over the rear of the garage. On my way up, I had to duck awkwardly under the power lines which stretched from a utility pole to the house, but the effort was worth it. I could see all around the house.

Right below me was a tiny strip of lawn, comfortably shaded by short, full trees. There was an old swing set, rusty from exposure and neglect and a smoke-blackened open pit brick barbecue. A sidewalk led from the rear of the house past a storm cellar door, then branched off in two directions. One path veered right at a ninety degree angle toward a wire gate. The other continued in a straight line away from the house. The rest of the outbuildings were partially blocked by a red-roofed stucco hut. Some noise I couldn't identify pulsed from inside the hut. It sounded kind of like a heartbeat, only amplified.

At The Cedars, we once had to read a story about a guy who kills an old man and buries his heart under the floorboards. The killer feels guilty, though, because he keeps hearing the old man's heart beating away. Nobody else hears it, and finally the killer goes crazy and admits he murdered his friend. For just one minute there, I pictured Mr. Skipworth was a killer who brought kids out to his farm and did away with them. That's right. I remembered Mr. Phelps telling me something about Mr. Skipworth's "helping" young kids.

So, okay, I admit it. I did sort of creep up on the little hut. And I looked behind the door before I walked all the way in. No vat of beating hearts, just a tack room with bridles and harnesses, tools everywhere, and five saddles hanging from cowhide strips. One saddle was a rich coppery color and it was tooled with all kinds of intricate designs. I almost felt like Clint Eastwood in those spaghetti westerns. But there was still the beating sound to deal with.

I followed the noise through another door, half expecting the ghosts of Mr. Skipworth's victims to rush me like a sacked quarterback. Instead, I saw an ancient water pump, thumping as it brought water from a deep shaft that ran through the floor of the room into the ground.

"She needs oil," observed Mr. Skipworth from the door of the tack room. If he noticed me jump back with surprise, he didn't let on. "Thought maybe you could do that for me."

"Sure thing, Mr. Skipworth. I knew she needed a lube job as soon as I heard her pumping away this morning. Where's the oil?" I asked, my voice a few octaves higher than usual.

Mr. Skipworth just smiled. "Well, Ross, I don't know how you could have missed it. You walked right by it. Nothing's bothering you, is it?" He smiled and I could tell he was getting a big bang out of watching me squirm. "You know," he said, "sometimes I think this old pump almost sounds like a beating heart." He laughed to himself and then whistled as he rummaged through some tools on the workbench.

Wordlessly, I followed him back into the other room where I found a little square can of oil. "Yeah," I nodded. "Here's just what I was looking for."

Mr. Skipworth handed me a set of wrenches and I followed him back into the pump house. After he cut the power to the pump, he told me to push my sleeve up over my shoulder to avoid getting caught in the mechanism. Then he explained how to get on my hands and knees, reach down, and check the threads on the bolts of the shaft's housing. Two of the bolts needed tightening, which wasn't easy given the way I had to perch, crab-like, over the hole as I fumbled for the wrench. Mr. Skipworth finally took pity on me and handed me the right tool—who knew *only* a 9/16ths socket, whatever that is, would do. Twice, I nearly dropped the wrench into the hole beneath me, but eventually, after a lot of clanking around and just as much cussing, I managed to tighten the bolts and grease the pump's shaft. I felt as though I'd done fifty pushups. With muscles quivering from unfamiliar use, I rolled over on my back and rubbed my biceps.

"Do you ever do anything fun around here?" I asked.

"Work first, fun later," Mr. Skipworth answered.

"What do you consider fun?" I said skeptically, "shoveling sh... uh, shoveling manure?"

"How about riding?" Mr. Skipworth said. "I keep several horses on the place."

I asked Mr. Skipworth how many horses he owned. With genuine pride, he gave me the complete rundown, starting with Beauty, his favorite.

"She's just about the prettiest horse I've ever owned," Mr. Skipworth boasted. "She's chestnut with a white star on her forehead. And she rides smooth as butter, too."

"Where's Beauty now?" I asked. "Could I see her?"

"Yep, soon as you're finished here, we'll get her down from the west pasture."

That was all the encouragement I needed to speed up the job on the pump. While I was cleaning a few careless oil spatters from the floor, Mr. Skipworth continued with his roster of horses.

"Bought several Shetlands a few years back. I wanted them for the grandkids. My family visits from the Midwest every August, you know." He was silent for a minute, sort of smiling to himself, before he continued. "Babe's the biggest of the string. Then there's Goldie and Tennessee." He laughed to himself. "Maybe you would like to try your hand with Lightning."

That sounded like a challenge too important to ignore. "You got him, I'll ride him," I bragged. I had never ridden before, and for all I knew, this Lightning could be a Brahma bull. Yet here I was, shooting off at the mouth.

"Lucky for you I won't hold you to that," observed Mr. Skipworth. "Come on. Let's get Beauty."

I followed Mr. Skipworth to the barn. Like a lot of

other things around the farm, the barn was in sad need of repair. Only a promise held the weathered gray slats together, and I knew I could plan on spending the next few thousand years painting and pounding nails. Still, there was no shame in the huge sign lettered with "Skip's Cedar Dell Ranch" in bold block print over the big hinged doors.

Mr. Skipworth led me to a room at the rear of the barn. He took a battered aluminum pan hanging from a nail off the wall and filled it with feed. As we retraced our steps to the barnyard, Mr. Skipworth let loose with a rapid series of piercing two-note whistles and called, "Come, Beauty. Come, girl." He poured half of the oats into one of the three concrete troughs and waited expectantly. Within minutes, a magnificent mare pranced around the far corner of the barn and trotted straight for the trough. Mr. Skipworth reached around under Beauty's neck and tugged affectionately at her mane.

"She *is* a beauty. Her name fits her," I said. The horse nickered, as if in agreement, before she gently nosed at the oats.

Mr. Skipworth headed for the tack room. "I'll just get the bridle," he called over his shoulder. "Give her the rest of the feed if you want."

I didn't have much choice. When Beauty finished with the oats in the trough, she turned full face to me and forced her muzzle into the aluminum pan.

Anxious to get every last bit of the meal, she kept pushing her nose further and further down until my forearms ached with effort to keep from dropping the pan. Actually, I was getting a little nervous about what would happen when the pan was empty. For all her gentleness, Beauty obviously had an enormous appetite, and I was beginning to worry she might like to try my fingers for dessert.

Mr. Skipworth returned, though, and with an ease that spoke of years of practice, he slipped the bit between Beauty's teeth and adjusted the leather strap of the bridle before buckling it securely around her head.

"You want to ride?" Mr. Skipworth asked.

"Are you kidding? You bet. Can we go now? Right away?"

"Might as well. I was going to drive you around the farm today anyway, but I don't see why we can't go on horseback," Mr. Skipworth agreed. "I'll get Babe. We'll pack a lunch and make a day of it." Mr. Skipworth instructed me to take Beauty and wait by the tack room.

It seemed to take forever before we had Babe, a large painted Shetland, saddled and tethered alongside Beauty. I had thrown together some peanut butter and jelly sandwiches and stuck some Fig Newtons in a paper bag. My pathetic lunch passed muster only because it would be carried in a genuine leather saddlebag on the back of my trusty steed. I couldn't wait to get started.

Mr. Skipworth claimed Beauty for himself. Babe was for me. At first I didn't care my horse was short and squat compared to Beauty. I mean, I was *mounted.* On a *horse.* But it didn't take long to find out Babe's gait was just awkward enough to make riding her for any length of time next to impossible. Every time I gave her any rein at all, I found myself coming down hard on the saddle, just as she was coming up. The jolt, multiplied by a thousand times over the course of the day, was enough to bring tears to the eyes of a jackhammer operator. The vision of me as a real-life range rider faded with every aching mile we traveled.

And did we travel! Sore or not, I have to admit Mr. Skipworth's farm had about everything in the world anyone could hope for. The scenery was spectacular. From the peak of the mountain at the rear of Mr. Skipworth's property we could see the rolling Ozark countryside for mile after mile. Rocky slopes met in little valleys, and farm ponds looked like liquid mercury reflecting the sun's rays. Mr. Skipworth told me he stocked one of his five ponds with bass, bluegill, and sunfish. I couldn't wait to get some fishing gear and throw a line in the water. At The Cedars, the closest we ever got to a fish fry was baked fish sticks served with a side of Tater Tots. Mr. Skipworth said I'd never taste anything like fish, fresh-caught from his pond, pan-fried and crispy. Ironically, even with the makings for a fish feast right at his fingertips, he said he didn't enjoy fishing at all. He said he didn't have the patience to sit around until some fish decided to take a chomp on his line. I promised to do enough fishing for the both of us if he would do the cooking.

It's funny the way we got along so well, especially considering we were practically strangers and less than twenty-four hours ago, I had made a solemn promise never to speak to Mr. Skipworth for the rest of my life. There was the age difference, too. I mean, I considered anyone over thirty-five as having one foot in the grave. By my reckoning, Mr. Skipworth was ready for the undertaker.

Somehow, though, I didn't care. Maybe it was because of the shop, or maybe there was so much to do on the farm I didn't have time to bother about the differences. Or maybe it was because those differences didn't matter to Mr. Skipworth. He knew what a hell-raiser I was and that I had been in plenty of trouble before, but he didn't pump me for information about my past. And he seemed to like me, really like *me*. It wasn't because I could do anything for him in return, either. We both knew I wasn't paying off my debt to Berryville, no matter how long I worked for Mr. Skipworth. He was bailing me out of a bad deal without expecting anything for it. I hadn't ever known anybody who did that, and it was a little hard getting used to. Sometimes I would catch myself looking for hidden meanings behind Mr. Skipworth's words or actions, but every time I started feeling resentful or suspicious, something would happen to make me laugh away my doubts.

That afternoon we ate our lunch on a bank by the Osage River. While the horses grazed, Mr. Skipworth took a nap under the shade of a huge cedar tree. I skipped a few stones until I got hot and went wading. The water was only about a foot and a half deep, so I just plopped down, clothes and all. When Mr. Skipworth woke up, I was still sitting in the river, the water gently swirling around my chest.

"Come on, Ross. Get out of there and try to dry off as best you can. I nearly forgot I promised Pres Scott I would help him ring his bull today."

"What's that mean, Mr. Skipworth?" I asked, stalling for more time in the river.

"Pres has a bull that's already a year old and he can't wean him. Should've been off the teat for nearly three months. We fix the bull so it can't suckle anymore. You'll see how it's done," he promised. "Maybe you can even help. It's kinda tricky business sometimes."

I hoped ringing the bull was really complicated and would take hours. The more time it took, the better. My rear end had taken such a pounding on Babe I felt like every muscle had been run through the durability test at Ford only to be stamped *REJECT*. My teeth even hurt. I wasn't going to let on to Mr. Skipworth, though. I set my jaw as we trotted off to Mr. Scott's spread.

We followed a narrow winding path hardly big enough for our two horses to walk side-by-side. The trail ended at a ramshackle house that looked no better than some of the condemned buildings I had seen in the poorest sections of Springfield, Missouri. Windows were broken out and ragged curtains hung limply in the afternoon stillness. The porch sagged in the middle, and several of the spindles in the wood railing had been broken in half or were missing altogether.

Mr. Skipworth's bellow brought Pres Scott from behind the house. He was as dilapidated and rundown as his property. He wore a soiled cotton shirt under baggy denim overalls and a wide-brimmed hat that pushed the tops of his ears forward. A grimy red bandana hung from his back pocket, although I don't know why he bothered to carry it. When he needed to blow his nose, he just ran his index finger and thumb down his nose and blew out with force. Then he would fling the snot off his fingers with a quick flick of his wrist. If that weren't bad enough, he offered that hand to me for a shake when Mr. Skipworth introduced us. Talk about a full-body shudder.

"Howdy, Luther. Pleased to meet y'all," he grinned at me. "Luther, glad you brung the boy along. I reckon he can he'p."

Mr. Skipworth slid easily from the saddle. "To be honest, Pres, I nearly forgot I promised to help you today. I was showing Ross around the place and we got a little sidetracked." The two men walked on around the house ahead of me. As they talked, they kept their voices low.

"I's in town late yeste'day afternoon," Pres was saying. "Heard tell you picked up another stray. How's this'n workin' out, Luther?"

"He's a good boy, Pres. Really a fine boy. Just had a few bad breaks, that's all. But he's a worker, he's willing, and he's curious about things." Mr. Skipworth's words almost made me forget how sore I was. I walked a little faster to catch up with the men.

"I took to him right away, Pres. Somehow Ross is different from those others. In fact, he kind of reminds me of myself. I think he'll work out fine."

"Well, you can't be none too careful, I alluz say," Pres snorted. "I kin remember when you thought the same way about them other boys, and you was disappointed. Mighty disappointed."

That really started me thinking. I didn't know Mr. Skipworth had tried to help guys like me before. Old Phelps hadn't said anything about that yesterday. Or did he? I remember him saying I wasn't the first kid who had ever messed up. Had Mr. Skipworth tried the same routine before? No wonder there hadn't been much of a stink when Mr. Skipworth offered to take me in. Still, Mr. Scott hinted those other times had ended in failure. I wondered what had gone wrong.

"Not this time, Pres," Mr. Skipworth said. "I'll not be disappointed this time. You'll see."

More than anything in the world, I wanted Mr. Skipworth to be right. Just this once, I thought, please let him be right.

Nine

Ditching an Attitude

"Ringing the bull" sounds like the title of a bad country-western song. Believe me, it was worse. It's the most gruesome thing I've ever seen.

I followed Pres and Mr. Skipworth to a barn about eighty yards from the house. Pres had positioned the bull, Honeyboy, in a narrow stall with his head poking between two movable slats facing the barn's center aisle. The bull was content for the moment because there was a full trough of feed smack under his nose. I suppose that's like giving a condemned man his last meal.

I ended up not helping at all because there was only room for one other person in the stall. Mr. Skipworth climbed over from the empty pen next to the bull and took his position right by Honeyboy's head. Mr. Skipworth wrapped his arms loosely around the bull's neck and planted his feet firmly against two sides of the tiny stall.

"Anytime you're ready, Pres," Mr. Skipworth announced.

"Okay, Luther. Give me room, boy."

I climbed over the rails of the stall opposite Mr. Skipworth and waited. Pres pulled out a piece of metal, a narrow rod curved in a U shape and filed to sharp points on both ends. He grabbed one of the bull's ears and pulled up.

"Now, Luther!"

Mr. Skipworth got a death grip on the bull's neck and braced himself against the stall. With a quick, hard jab, Pres drove one end of the rod into the left side of the bull's nose. I heard a sickening pop as the rod pierced the cartilage and poked through the other side. I couldn't tell if there was much blood because I turned my head away just then. When I looked back, Pres had let go of the bull's ear and grabbed onto the two ends of the rod. Honeyboy didn't move an inch with that thing through his nose.

"That's a good job done, heh, Pres?" Mr. Skipworth said. "Went much easier than a lot I've done before."

"I'll be damned, it sure did," agreed Pres. "Now we'll just finish 'im up. Would you get the mallet from my workbench over there, boy?"

God, what more could they do to that bull? I handed the mallet to Pres a little reluctantly. Using the handle of the mallet for leverage, Mr. Scott bent the two prongs of metal upward, so Honeyboy looked something like the warthogs I had seen pictured in books about Africa. Only this time, the tusks were made of metal and the bull was bleeding through the nose. He kept snorting and shaking his head and stamping his feet.

"Well, let's see how he works," Pres said. He opened the stall and Honeyboy bolted into the adjoining corral. Pres followed him and tried to slap him affectionately on the rear, but Honeyboy was having none of it. I figured it would be a good long time before Pres—or anyone else, for that matter—would be able to get within five hundred feet of him.

"How long is he going to hurt?" I asked.

Pres snorted at my ignorance. "Aw, he don't hurt none. 'S only jes a little nuisance, that's all."

"Easy for you to say," I muttered under my breath. I don't think Mr. Scott heard me, but I know Mr. Skipworth did.

"That's enough, Ross. We should be getting home."

"Thankee, Luther, for your he'p," said Pres. "Y'all take care and don't be strangers."

"See you soon, Pres," answered Mr. Skipworth. He looked at me like he was waiting for me to say something, but I silently mounted Babe and turned her head toward home. Mr. Skipworth was obviously upset I was so rude to his friend, especially since he had bragged about how I was so different from the other boys he had taken in. He took special care to let Pres know *we* were happy to help and to call on *us* again for anything. Mr. Skipworth climbed up on Beauty and followed me.

We rode along for a minute or so in silence. I was expecting a lecture, but I didn't get one. Mr. Skipworth just pointed in the distance.

"Look over yonder, Ross. See that bull?"

Honeyboy was trying to suckle another cow, a full-uddered heifer followed by a wobbly-legged calf. Every time Honeyboy nudged the heifer, the sharp tips of the metal rod forced her to kick and move away. Finally Honeyboy gave up, moved off, and started to graze. The cow allowed her calf to nurse, though. Mr. Skipworth smiled.

"See, Ross? Now things are the way they should be."

"Okay," I said, "but, sooner or later, wouldn't Honeyboy wean himself?"

"Pres didn't have time to wait for nature to take its course. We just gave Honeyboy an easy little shove in the right direction."

"Easy if you're not Honeyboy," I shot back.

"Here's the thing, Ross. I know you don't much like what happened back there, but sometimes the ways of the world tilt off kilter. When that happens, we have to jump in and take charge. Just because you don't like the methods doesn't mean they're wrong."

"Maybe," I conceded, "but do the methods have to be so cruel? That wasn't much fun to watch."

"Lots of things seem cruel," agreed Mr. Skipworth. "But that's the way of the world, and you better get used to the facts. You can bet you'll brush up against your share of hard times—and they'll be a lot harder than watching Pres and me ring that bull. The thing is, when you find yourself up against something rough, you just have to make a choice. Are you going to deal with it? Are you going to sit back and do nothing? All the worrying and second guessing won't change your situation. It only wastes time." He got a little philosophical then. "I deal with the things that are in my power to deal with. I let the rest of them go, Ross. Just let the rest of them go."

The road home seemed shorter than I expected, somehow. I guess I was too busy thinking about ringing the bull to care about how much Babe was bouncing me around in the saddle. Maybe that's why I had a little accident.

Babe was getting pretty frisky when we rounded that last bend before turning off the gravel road onto the shoulder of the highway leading to the farm. She knew a long day of exercising was just about over, and I imagine she was as anxious to get me off her back as I was to get off. Unfortunately, her schedule and mine didn't exactly coincide. I wasn't paying attention and had given her too much rein. When I relaxed my grip, she broke into a full gallop. I was so surprised I didn't have time to react. Babe sent me spinning, butt over brain, into the ditch at the side of the road. There was little enough to cushion my fall and absolutely nothing to cushion my pride.

"You okay, boy?" Mr. Skipworth asked.

"Do I look okay?" I snarled.

"You look... uh... you look..." He couldn't finish. The corner of his mouth turned up. He tried covering up, but it wasn't working. A little smirk grew into a full-out howl. He laughed like a hyena until I thought he was going to keel over and land beside me in the ditch.

"Cut it out," I yelled. "It's not funny. I could've been killed."

Mr. Skipworth was doubled over. Then he sat up and threw his head back. "Ah—hee—hee—hee." He was snorting and laughing so hard he could barely breathe.

"You should see your face," he gasped.

Very few people at The Cedars ever got away with making fun of me. I wasn't used to being laughed at. Usually I'd get this kind of hot feeling in my stomach that just seemed to explode to my fists, and I'd end up swinging. I remember one time in particular at The Cedars when I spent two weeks under house arrest for fighting. A really annoying newcomer, Dean Burris, was trying to build a rep for himself. He must have decided I'd be an easy target because I was too small to be much of a threat. He started calling me by my last name, like most of the guys at The Cedars did, but he'd say "Bein' a *dick*" instead of "Benedict." I'd taken his mouth for a couple of days, but one morning at breakfast I waited for him to walk by my table in the cafeteria. I tripped him, watched him sprawl face first in his scrambled eggs and then I pounced on him. When the counselors pulled me off him, the grape jelly smeared in his hair matched the color of the bruise darkening his left eye.

For some reason, though, this time I didn't fly off like I usually do. I sort of imagined I was on Beauty with Mr. Skipworth, looking down at myself sprawled on the ground. I guess I did look sort of funny. I started chuckling and shaking my head. Then I laughed, laughed so hard I nearly wet my pants. Anyone who would have seen us just then, hooting and howling like that, would have taken us for a couple of loonies.

Mr. Skipworth composed himself enough to reach down. "Climb up, Ross. Babe's probably home by now."

I briefly rested my forehead against Beauty's flank before I scrambled up behind Mr. Skipworth. My limp arms slipped around him, and we managed to make it home without any more mishaps.

Sometimes you look back and say *this* was a day that mattered. That Sunday mattered. I'd always been known at The Cedars as a tough guy, ready to punch out anyone who pissed me off. If you dared to laugh at me, watch out.

Mr. Skipworth had laughed. Loud. Unstoppable. Directed right at me, at how foolish I looked there in the ditch. And I had laughed too. I guess my temper wasn't on automatic pilot. I could change.

Changes don't come easy, though. It's tough trying to control gut reactions, especially when the first instinct is to fight. There were so many times after that Sunday Mr. Skipworth egged me on, just to see how much I could take. He would push me too far, and I'd end up hitting my fist into the wall, or storming off, or saying the raunchiest things I could think of. Still, after the incident with Babe, I wasn't quite so quick to pull the trigger. Mr. Skipworth seemed to know when to back off and let me rage. He also knew when to tell me to "man yourself up," his favorite way of saying stop acting like a dumb kid.

Both of us were ready to collapse that night. After we raided the icebox, we sat watching some third-rate western and waiting for the ten o'clock news to come on. Neither one of us made it, though. Mr. Skipworth was out after a few minutes, and I must have followed suit right after that. When I woke up, there was a tiny bright dot on the center of the screen and a lot of static—some of it from the TV set, some of it from Mr. Skipworth's snoring. I didn't even bother to click off the set. I just punched the pillow on the sofa a couple of times and went back to sleep.

Ten

Chocolates and Choices

Things started settling into a routine on Monday. Because Mr. Skipworth worked every Saturday, his weekends fell on Sunday and Monday. Monday was his day to take the pickup into town and load the big box of clipped hair from the shop onto the truck. Later in the day he would drive to a ditch at the rear of his property and dump the box along with the rest of the week's trash. We also took care of a lot of business in town. We stopped at Hanby's feed store to buy salt blocks for the cattle and feed for the horses. Mr. Skipworth checked the mail at the post office, paid a few bills, and stopped to visit with several people moving around the town square. Most of their talk involved me and the fountain because crews had already started to drain the basin and begin the clean-up operation.

I figured all the fuss was pretty rough on Mr. Skipworth. He had to listen to the old-timers and their dire observations about "this damn younger generation," and I was their poster boy.

"... don't know why you even bother, Luther. Isn't he like all the others?"

"Yeah? Well, if was up to me, I tell you exactly what I'd do with them punks at that school..."

"Are you sure you can trust him out there on the property? You're a ways from town and..."

Through all of this, Mr. Skipworth made no comment. He didn't defend my actions and he didn't make excuses for me. I hated having him listen to all their garbage. Finally, I just started hanging back, out of earshot. That didn't stop most of the old coots, though. They kept gesturing in my direction and shaking their heads. When I look back on it now, I think that public ridicule was Mr. Skipworth's way of testing the limits of my self-control. He was pushing me, daring me to blow up. I kept quiet, even though I wanted to tell every last one of them where to stick it. In his own good time, Mr. Skipworth put a stop to all the talk.

"Well, if it was me, I'd watch my back and lock up everything worth anything," one old guy was saying.

Mr. Skipworth interrupted right then. "Excuse me." He turned to me and announced loudly, "Come on, Ross. Let's get on home with this load." He planted a hand firmly on my shoulder and we walked over to the truck without another word. I think it was his way of saying I didn't need to be ashamed to face anybody in town for any reason.

In the weeks that followed, I had plenty of opportunity to meet folks in Berryville. Mr. Skipworth started depending more and more on me to run errands. If the shoeshine business was a little slow, he'd send me to Carr's Dry Goods or the post office. Sometimes I'd deliver one of Mr. Skipworth's books to a friend or a customer. Then, a few weeks later I'd have to go back and pick it up. All the odd jobs came to me. If I needed a tool or gadget for a repair job, Mr. Skipworth would trust me to take money from the cash register and return the change when I got back. Sometimes I would run over to Check's or Garner's Drive-In for hamburgers and sodas, and we would eat our lunches in the shop together.

If I wasn't running some errand or other, I'd meet people in the shop. By following Mr. Skipworth's lead, I found out how to handle those customers who didn't take to me right away. I'd just sit back and listen to them talk. No man who ever entered a barber shop can resist talking as long as there's a willing listener, and no subject was off limits. In fact, I learned more in those weeks than I had in five years of formal education at The Cedars. My barbershop professors discussed stock and feed, agriculture, market prices, economics, government, the weather, education, and Agatha Beasmore, a seventy-two-year-old spinster who dyed her hair black and drove a red convertible.

Everything considered, life away from The Cedars suited me. About the only job I dreaded was writing letters to Mr. Skipworth's sisters for him. When he told me to write that first letter, I couldn't believe it. Of course, I never got any mail at The Cedars, so I'm no expert. But I still figured letters should be personal and private, especially family letters.

One afternoon, out of the blue, he said, "Get some of that fancy paper out of the desk. I want you to write to my sister Lena." He might as well have said, "Take those dirty towels into the back room and wash them in the bathtub." It wasn't a request open for debate. He explained the personal details I was supposed to include in the letter, like asking about Lena's bursitis and whether or not her neighbor's pup had thrown her litter yet. Then he said I could add anything I wanted to about the weather in Berryville or what was happening around the farm.

I had no idea how I was going to explain why I was writing instead of Mr. Skipworth. I mean, how could I explain something I didn't even understand? I must have wasted about a ream of paper before I decided I wasn't going to do any explaining. I just wrote the letter like I thought Mr. Skipworth wanted and I signed his name. Writing *Luther* at the bottom of the page felt funny, but I figured his sisters could spend their time puzzling over why Mr. Skipworth's handwriting had suddenly changed. In their letters, they never mentioned anything about the unfamiliar handwriting. We left it at that.

Mr. Skipworth wrote his own letters to Jorita, his only daughter, though, and he never told me what he said to her about my living out at the farm. If I asked what she thought about me, Mr. Skipworth just said I'd get a chance to meet her later in the summer. He didn't seem too concerned, so I didn't press the issue.

Other than being saddled with chores I hated, like letter writing—oh, and maybe washing towels in the bathtub in the back room—I felt like I belonged in Mr. Skipworth's world. People were always stopping by the shop, and the regular customers started calling me *Ross* and *son* with real warmth in their voices. The citizens of Berryville seemed to forgive me for the fountain almost as quickly as they condemned me.

I also found plenty of excuses to make frequent trips to the Berryville Drug for chocolate sodas and quick, often interrupted talks with Sara Greenwoldt. What started as curiosity about my bad-boy image developed into real friendship. I think we might even have dated if things had turned out differently.

Indirectly, in fact, Sara first made me think about school in the fall. I guess I sort of thought summer would stretch on forever, and I would just go on running errands and shining shoes indefinitely. Sara, like everyone else in town, knew my arrangement with Mr. Skipworth was temporary until the fountain business was taken care of. Unlike everyone else in town, Sara didn't automatically assume I'd go back to The Cedars once school started.

"You mean you haven't even registered for the first term yet?" she asked. "Being a new student, you would get the first crack at all the good classes. You could even register before the seniors."

"I… well… I guess I'll just be going back to The Cedars. My records are there along with everything else."

"Who are you kidding?" Sara demanded. "Nothing is there. Nothing that matters."

"What about my friends?" I countered.

"Funny you haven't been hauling your cookies out to The Cedars to hang out with them before this," she said. "You can make all kinds of friends at High. Besides, they probably won't get you into the kind of trouble you had out there."

I got a little defensive, although I'm not sure why. "A leopard doesn't change its spots, Sara. I'll always be what I am right now."

"If that's the way you see yourself, then maybe you're right. Maybe you *ought* to go back to The Cedars. What's your name for the place—Loser

Central?" Her voice was like steel. "Excuse me. I've got to wash out some sundae dishes."

She was right, of course. I'd kill to begin the fall semester at High and go on working with Mr. Skipworth after school. I didn't know how I was going to swing it, but I was sure going to try. Maybe I could stay with Mr. Skipworth for awhile if Mr. Phelps, that guy from the county, could find some way to make it happen. The first chance I got, I promised myself, I'd feel out Mr. Skipworth on the subject.

Leaving my soda half finished, I wandered out of the drugstore toward the shop. I made a U-turn, though, and bought a box of chocolates with the soft crème centers. They were Mr. Skipworth's favorites, and I figured it wouldn't hurt my cause any to buy a little insurance.

The shop was quiet when I walked in. Only the whirring fan and the rustle of Mr. Skipworth's paper broke the silence.

"I brought you some chocolates, Mr. Skipworth. You like the soft centers, don't you?"

"That's mighty nice," he said. He examined the little paper chart in the top of the box before selecting an orange crème. He ate two more pieces before he thought to offer me one.

"No," I said. "They're all for you."

"I'm glad for them. Thanks. Why don't you put the rest of them in the icebox in the back. I'm afraid they'll be a gooey mess if I leave them in this heat too long. But be sure to remind me to take them back out to the house this evening. I wouldn't want to forget them." I walked to the back room and stuck the box away in the fridge.

"Ross," Mr. Skipworth said when I returned, "I've been meaning to talk with you about something. Do you have a little time?"

"Yes, sir," I answered. This was obviously not the time to bring up my plan to Mr. Skipworth. Something was troubling him.

"I have a proposition to make, and I'd be a liar if I said this came out of anything but my own self-interest."

My stomach turned to Jell-O. Whatever his plan was didn't sound too good for me.

"Ross, you know you've more than paid for the cost of the fountain repairs, don't you?"

"I didn't really keep track, Mr. Skipworth," I said. "I figured you would tell me when I'd worked off my debt."

"Well, then, I'll get to the point," he said.

I couldn't ask questions fast enough. "What's wrong? What's the matter? What are you trying to say?"

"You've worked off your debt. You don't owe me anything anymore, and as far as anyone knows, you could head back out to the school whenever you want."

I flinched.

"Is that what you want, boy? Are you wanting to go back out to The Cedars?"

"Mr. Skipworth," I began, but he interrupted before I could finish.

"You know, my sisters have accused me of being a selfish man, Ross," Mr. Skipworth was saying. "They may be right. I guess only time will tell."

"What does being selfish have to do with anything?" I demanded.

"I want to retain a lawyer, Ross. I want him to begin working on papers that will allow you to stay with me on the farm right on through the fall and winter and beyond. If you're willing, that is."

"I… I… "

"I know, Ross, I know," broke in Mr. Skipworth. "I shouldn't have sprung that on you all at once. It's only right you have time to think on it awhile. After all, I'm an old man. That will matter more and more as time goes on. I'll have to turn a good part of the responsibility for the place over to you, and that's no small consideration. It may be you don't want that kind of burden. And there are other things to deal with, too. Lots of other things. For now, though, just think on it. Take your time and think. When you're ready, then we'll talk."

"When I'm ready?" I laughed. "Are you kidding? I brought you those chocolates to soften you up. I thought it would make it easier to ask about living on the farm for awhile. Do we think with the same brain? We must, because here you are, offering me the answer to something I could never ask for." I shook my head in disbelief. "And you tell me to take my time? The answer is yes, Mr. Skipworth, definitely YES."

"Whoa, son," Mr. Skipworth said. "Slow down. Do you know what saying 'yes' really means to you? To me?"

"I know it means I'd go to school at High. It means I'd get to live on the farm and work at the shop. It means I'd be the first kid my age that ever left The Cedars for something better than juvie detention center." I was on a roll. "It means I don't have to feel like a loser, like a throwaway reject."

"That covers you," Mr. Skipworth observed wryly, "but why do you think *I'm* asking? I told you, I've been called a selfish man."

"Well…," I hesitated. "I guess you want some help on the farm and at the shop."

"True," he said, "but you could help me without living with me."

"Yeah," I agreed. "Then why *are* you doing this?"

"I want you to be my Tobe McKinney," he said. "I want you to be my second chair."

"Right," I answered. "That means nothing to me. Who's Tobe McKinney? What's a second chair?"

"I've barbered here for more than fifty years, Ross. Even though I work alone now, two other men used to be here with me, working alongside me every day. Tobe McKinney cut hair for me for years, and he barbered in the second chair. This chair." He gestured at the barber chair next to him. "He was my worker, but he was also my friend," Mr. Skipworth explained. "We counted on each other. We took care of each other. I knew when I needed him, he'd be right there."

"And you think you can count on me, too?" I asked.

"I think I can count on you. I think I can count on you for a long time to come."

"How long is a long time?" I asked. "This year? Until I graduate?"

"Longer," Mr. Skipworth said. "Until I die."

Eleven

File # ARN641110508

Being elected President of the United States has to be easier than being adopted. I had been living with Mr. Skipworth for almost two months now, and nobody had so much as blinked. As soon as we wanted to make the living arrangements legal, everybody wanted to get into the act. I saw the inside of a courtroom more than Perry Mason, and I answered more questions than a contestant on *Jeopardy*. I think I learned enough about adoption laws in Arkansas to be admitted to the bar.

The procedure was really involved. After Mr. Skipworth hired a lawyer, I assumed most of the work would be out of our hands. No way. Mr. Skipworth had to file something called a Petition to Adopt, which asked general background questions like name, age, place of residence, and so on. Then the questions got more personal. According to Mr. Skipworth, some of the information required on the petition was "nobody's damn business," but we answered the questions anyway.

I had to ask the authorities at The Cedars to look up information about my natural parents. As I've said, my mom was just a teenager, seventeen, when she had me. My father was three years older, originally from Tahlequah, Oklahoma, according to the records. He bolted before I was born, leaving my mom to decide my fate. And that, as they say, is history. Foster homes. Lots of foster homes. With each transfer to yet another host family, my prospects for adoption fell off the grid. It's like being a box of cereal. The longer you sit on the shelf, the more important the expiration date becomes. After I was in the system for so long, nobody wanted to take a chance with stale goods. Eventually, I wasn't even getting foster home placements, so The Cedars was the end of the line. Hard to believe I was used up at ten years old. I'm kind of surprised, in fact, everyone at the school seemed willing to help with all the paperwork. I'm pretty sure they believed a long-time resident like me would never go up for adoption. Don't get me wrong. I was thankful and all, but I didn't plan on sending them any Hallmark cards or anything.

After The Cedars submitted the background information, Mr. Skipworth and I had to write a long paper explaining how I came to live with him. We listed about a thousand reasons why we thought the adoption would be a good move. Because I was over fourteen, Arkansas law also required my formal consent to the proposed adoption. Finally, after the lawyer recorded the necessary papers, we were ready to meet with a judge.

On the day of the hearing, Mr. Skipworth and I drove into town earlier than usual. He made the motions of cleaning the shop even though we both knew neither of us would be able to work, no matter what the outcome. At nine-thirty, we walked over to the courthouse and made our way to the chambers of the honorable Judge Ernst Carter. Mr. Skipworth had told me not to wear a tie. The situation wasn't that formal, he said, and I might as well be comfortable. Mr. Skipworth looked like he always did. He was wearing his usual uniform—slacks and suspenders, starched white shirt and tie. Calm as he tried to appear, he couldn't keep his fingers from shaking as he ran them nervously around the brim of his hat.

I was surprised to find Sheriff Stoner waiting in the judge's chambers. For awhile, I thought he had come to throw a wrench into the works. Even though we'd run into each other several times since early June and the words we exchanged were civil enough, I still remembered his old threats. I half expected him to try screwing this up for Mr. Skipworth and me. As it turned out, he was present at the request of the review board from The Cedars. He had brought a signed Document of Consent, just another of the required papers, because my legal guardian—the head man at The Cedars—couldn't make the hearing himself.

The proceedings were a little disappointing. I had imagined myself, eloquent and fiery, pleading our case in front of a jury. Mr. Skipworth's role was to sit wistfully in the background, looking hopeful but uncertain. Instead, I might as well have been a piece of furniture. Judge Carter barely looked in my direction, much less asked me to say a few words on behalf of the adoption request. He simply shuffled through the stack of documents and made the astute observation, "Everything seems to be in order." He asked about only one item on the application.

"I see you've neglected to enter any religious affiliation, sir." Judge Carter peered over his reading glasses at Mr. Skipworth.

"That's correct, your honor," said Mr. Skipworth. "If you have to list something, you can put 'atheist' in the blank."

"I see," Judge Carter replied. "Am I to assume you might attempt to influence the boy to pursue the same path you have chosen?"

"Ross may do as he pleases, sir," Mr. Skipworth answered. "He's a bright young man with a good mind. If he wants formal religious training, that's for him to decide. I wouldn't try to influence him one way or the other. He has to find what's true for him."

"I respect that, sir," the judge nodded slowly. "And I know your word is your bond. I'm afraid, however, Mr. Skipworth, the State Department of Public Welfare may not be as understanding."

"Again, sir?" Neither Mr. Skipworth nor I understood the judge.

"I mean, Mr. Skipworth, even if *I* deem this proposed adoption to be in the best interests of all involved parties, there is still one further step before the final adoption decree is issued."

"What would that step be, sir?"

"I have to grant an Interlocutory Decree. In effect, that stops the proceedings while the court conducts a more thorough investigation. Social workers from the Child Welfare Division of the State Department of Public Welfare will visit you and Ross in your home, Mr. Skipworth. I give you fair warning your lack of religious affiliation will not help your cause. When you couple that with the unusually large differences in ages between you and the boy, the success of this adoption looks rather bleak to me." He paused before adding, somewhat sympathetically, I thought, "If it were within my power, I would approve this petition without hesitation. I wish you both good luck. I'm afraid you'll need it."

That was that. Judge Carter formally granted the

Interlocutory Decree and made arrangements for the social workers to visit us a few times in the coming months. He told us a six-month waiting period was required by law before a final decree could be issued. In the meantime, I could go on living with Mr. Skipworth and make plans to register at High for the fall term.

Only one little cloud darkened my day. I was worried about Judge Carter's reservations. The religion thing didn't bother me much. If the social workers couldn't see Mr. Skipworth had integrity and lived by moral principles (whether he called it religion or not didn't matter), well, then, they were blind and stupid.

The age difference was altogether different, though. Mr. Skipworth's lawyer had said most adopting parents are anywhere from twenty to forty years older than the kids they adopt. Anything outside those guidelines would be cause for concern. Mr. Skipworth was about to celebrate his seventy-fifth birthday, which would make him sixty years older than me. I was afraid those welfare people who didn't know Mr. Skipworth might think he was just an old man. Would they penalize him just because he had lived longer than other people? I decided when the social workers paid their visits to us, I wasn't going to keep quiet like I did during the hearing. In fact, I could almost hear Mr. Skipworth's voice echoing in my head *When you find yourself up against something rough, you just have to make a choice. Are you going to deal with it? Are you going to sit back and do nothing?*

If I had to, I would threaten to get into real trouble if the adoption didn't go through. I'd tell those social workers and the judge and anyone else who would listen that without Mr. Skipworth my life would be in the toilet and I'd probably end up in prison or dead. Who wants that on their conscience?

This would work. It had to work. Mr. Skipworth was the best thing that had ever happened to me, and I think I was good for him, too. Somehow, the social workers and the judge would agree to that. If they did, well, my life would be perfect.

Twelve

Family Ties

So what changed after the hearing? Not much, except I started calling Mr. Skipworth "Mr. S." Even though Judge Carter had legally linked our names on an official-looking document, we treated each other the same way we had since day one at the shop. Now, though, we knew there was the promise of a permanence neither one of us could have ever expected.

The news was too big to keep to myself. I had to tell Sara right away. After all, she'd been supportive, a real friend, right from the beginning. In a rare fit of generosity, I offered to buy a round of chocolate sodas at the Berryville Drug. Mr. Skipworth, for once, didn't hurry back to open the shop.

As soon as Sara saw my face, she knew Judge Carter had given us the green light. I swear, her smile matched mine. In a not-so-rare fit of generosity, Sara refused to charge me for the sodas.

"My treat, Ross. I'm really happy for both of you. We'll have to get together and talk about some of your classes at High. Maybe I can answer some questions about teachers and courses and stuff."

"Great," I agreed. "Maybe later this week. I'll talk to you."

"Be sure you do," Sara said. "I need to get back to work. Bye, Ross. Congratulations, Mr. Skipworth."

We finished our sodas slowly. As I was slurping the last of mine, Mr. S reminded me he still had one person left to tell.

"I need to call Jorita," he announced. "She'll want to hear the news."

To be honest, I had almost forgotten about Mr. S's only daughter. She knew about the petition, and according to Mr. S, she hadn't said much one way or the other. If I had been in her shoes, though, I don't really think I'd be too hot to gain an adopted brother nearly forty years younger. She called regularly, and I knew she was planning to visit the first week in August to celebrate Mr. S's birthday, just like always, but I didn't have a clue about her take on all this adoption business.

I was nervous as hell about meeting her. How would she react to me? What would I say? With a start, I realized I'd better come up with a game plan pretty soon. This was Wednesday, and she would be in Berryville on Saturday night.

When I tried to ask Mr. S what to expect, he just laughed. "You can expect we have plenty to do before the family comes to town. Every room in the house needs a good going-over, especially the kitchen."

I had to admit, any woman would have a hemorrhage at the way we kept house. In this case, we would have to pass inspection from no fewer than four females. Jorita had three daughters, Karen, Jan, and Pam. The oldest two, Karen and Jan, were married and had four kids between them. Pam was still "lovin' 'em and leavin' 'em," according to her mother.

Mr. S called Jorita the minute we returned to the shop. He delivered the news, paused, shook his head, and said something softly into the receiver. The rest of the conversation lasted only a few minutes, just long enough for her to explain the travel plans. The family should leave Iowa early Saturday, drive all day, and arrive in Berryville before we closed the shop.

"What did she say?" I asked. "Is she okay with the decision?"

Mr. S answered, "You'll meet her. She'll meet you. Then we'll see." Not particularly reassuring, I thought.

Yesterday I had been a ward of the state. By the weekend, I would face my new, instant family. My head was spinning.

The rest of the week cruised by, probably because

Mr. S and I were so busy. Besides the work at the shop, we had mountains to move at the farm. We washed all the bedding and aired the pillows out on the line behind the house. I moved my gear out to the sleeping porch beyond Mr. S's room so my bedroom would be available. We dusted furniture and knocked cobwebs from the corners of the ceilings. I found an old canister vacuum in the back of the linen closet in the hallway and did the best I could with the carpets. When we finished, the place was cleaner than it had ever been since I showed up at the farm. I wanted the family to think Mr. S and I made out all right together.

For all my anticipation and preparation, I was a basket case by Saturday. Time crawled by so slowly I wondered if someone kept setting the clocks back. Unlike most Saturdays, we were less busy than usual. Fewer customers meant more idle time, something neither of us needed. We pretended to look busy as long as we could before we finally settled into the barber chairs and admitted our anxiety.

To distract us, Mr. S shared memories from past visits. He told me he used to keep the grandkids occupied by saddling one of the Shetlands and leading the pony into the back yard. He would tie the reins from the bridle to one arm of the revolving clothesline and then attach the horse's tail to another arm of the clothesline. The grandkids could ride the horseshoes off the Shetland as the pony walked in circles, Mr. S wouldn't wear out his boots leading the pony all over the farm, and everybody was happy—except maybe the horse.

He also remembered the time he tried to teach his granddaughters one of his favorite maxims: Learn by doing. He thought they ought to know the chicken they ate for dinner didn't simply appear in the supermarket, magically packaged in shrink-wrap. Once, he recalled, he butchered hens, insisting the girls help him every step of the way. He chopped off the heads of the chickens, but their pulsing nerves kept the birds flopping around for awhile. "Green," he laughed. "Faces really can turn green." Karen lasted the longest, scalding and plucking the hens. Jan ditched, complaining of a sick stomach, and Pam got all bent out of shape because she had named every one of the chickens. He said none of the girls spoke a civil word to him for the rest of that vacation.

My favorite story was when Mr. S took his granddaughters frog hunting at his pond across the highway. Duke, a German Shepherd Mr. S owned before Geraldine, had gone along, but she stubbornly ignored Mr. S's command to retrieve anything from the algae-covered water. In the end, Karen waded in gingerly to pull the frogs to shore. Then Jan took over, poking a sharpened stick through their bellies. She carried the slimy catch, their bodies slapping together with every step, all the way home.

Mr. S recalled memory after memory until the afternoon sun sent lengthening shadows through the shop. He looked at his watch frequently and told me to watch for a little girl, Karen's daughter, Michele. Every year, he said, the family sent his great-granddaughter into the shop before the rest of the troop burst through the doors. She would wander in a little uncertainly, and Mr. S would pretend he didn't recognize her. Finally, he'd open his eyes in mock surprise and exclaim he never in the world expected to see her showing up on his doorstep. The week-long vacation would be officially underway.

I loved hearing those stories and I envied the special, familiar little routines Mr. S described. I found myself wondering what it might be like to make memories of my own with my new family. That made waiting for their arrival all the harder.

Thirteen

In or Out?

About a quarter to six, a pretty, golden-haired little girl stepped into the shop. Her clothes were wrinkled and her footing a little unsure. Mr. S. winked at me before turning his full attention to the girl.

"Yes, young lady? What can I do for you? Is it a haircut you want, or did you come in for a shave?" He ushered her to his barber's chair and picked her up.

"I don't want a shave," she protested.

"No?" he chuckled.

"No, Papa. Don't you know me?" The little girl didn't seem too pleased with the turn of events.

"Can't say as I do," Mr. S kidded.

Just then, the rest of the family burst through the doors, everyone talking at once.

"Hi, Granddad."

"Daddy!"

"Say 'hi' to Papa."

"Did you recognize Michele, Granddad?"

Mr. S hugged each of his granddaughters in succession. He lifted his great-grandkids high over his head and shook hands with Curt and Rick, Karen and Jan's husbands. His son-in-law, Vernon, slapped Mr. S on the back and commented about the stifling heat. With Jorita, though, Mr. S lingered the longest. He stood with his arm around his daughter's shoulders, looking proudly at his tribe.

I had waited so long to meet this group that starred in Mr. S's stories, but I was suddenly uncomfortable. I felt like someone who had wandered into the room by accident, an uninvited guest who had crashed a private party. Whether the adoption went through or not wouldn't make any difference. I was extra baggage. A piece of paper wasn't going to make me a part of this group, no matter badly I wanted it. Even Mr. S seemed to have forgotten me as he joked with his family.

Bored with all the talk, Bryan, Jan's four-year-old son, eyed me from safely behind his mother's leg. A couple of times, he pulled on her shorts and pointed silently at me. Unsatisfied with her reassuring little pat on the head, Bryan pulled more insistently. "Who's that, Momma?"

"Bryan, this is Ross," Jan explained. "Can you say hello?"

Bryan shook his head and wrapped both arms

around Jan's leg, anchoring himself to safety.

I knelt down to his level and did the only thing I could think of that might intrigue a little kid. I flipped my upper eyelids back on themselves, and sucked in my cheeks. I put my hands on either side of my head and waved them back and forth like the gills on a fish. Bryan's eyes widened, and if he could have become invisible, he would have. Instead, he made himself as small as possible by folding his arms in front of his chest and turning sideways behind his mother. Michele giggled.

Jorita, who had been watching the whole exchange, caught my eye, broke away from Mr. S and approached me. "Ross, I'm glad to finally meet you."

I rose, putting my hand out for her to shake. She took it and held it briefly before pulling me toward her for a hug. Awkwardly, I lifted my arms around her. Before she released me, she whispered in my ear, "I hope the two of us have a chance to visit." I stepped back, nodding my head stupidly.

"Ross and I have been anxious for you to get here," Mr. S said.

"I give you fair warning," Jorita replied, "you may wish you were someplace else after this horde has been here for a couple of days."

She made the introductions, but I already knew everyone from Mr. S's descriptions. Michele, the blonde little six-year-old, belonged to Karen and Curt.

Rick and Jan had three sons, eighteen-month-old twins Greg and Chad and their older brother Bryan. The boys all resembled their parents, with dark hair and big brown eyes. Michele, fair-skinned and green-eyed, was just the opposite. Mr. Skipworth's youngest granddaughter, Pam, sported a rock on her hand that announced her engagement to a guy back in Iowa. Apparently her "love 'em and leave 'em" days would soon be over.

"The wedding's in December," Pam was saying. "You're going to come, aren't you, Granddad?"

"Well, if I can get away. It's hard to leave the place with no one to look after it," Mr. S answered.

"Wrong answer, Daddy," Jorita cut in. "If you can head to South Dakota to see some random fossil and trek to Mexico to look at Aztec ruins, I think you can arrange to come to your granddaughter's wedding." She seemed to be joking, but there was an unmistakable edge to her voice that made Karen and Jan exchange glances. "Besides," Jorita continued, "you don't want to play favorites, do you? You managed to leave the shop when Karen and Jan got married."

"Yeah," Pam joked, "but we all understand what momentous occasions *those* were. Who knew *anyone* would be willing to marry Karen and Jan?"

Rick and Curt hooted their agreement and Rick made some comment about their being nominated for sainthood. "If we didn't marry them," he said, elbowing Curt, "they'd end up as old maid spinsters who dye their hair purple."

"Yeah," Karen shot back. "Could we be any more blessed?" She made a mock gagging gesture and then they all broke up in laughter.

"Back to the wedding," Pam insisted. "Make him come, Ross. If you two don't show up in tuxedos, I'll never speak to you again."

"Maybe the Thomasons can take you to Springfield to catch a plane. Then we can drive you back after the wedding, Daddy." Jorita was already making plans. "I'll probably need a week's rest anyway, once this shindig is all over."

"We'll see," was the only commitment Mr. S would make, but I figured even Mr. S wouldn't be able to deny four women with wedding plans on the brain. Now, in addition to starting at High, I might have a trip north and a family event to look forward to. Before Mr. S happened, I never remembered looking any farther than the next day.

Mr. S decided to close the shop right away. He told the family to go on out to the farm and unload while we swept up. They all piled into their cars and waved and honked as they made their way around the square and toward the highway.

"I like them," I told Mr. S. "I like them a lot."

"Tell me that at the end of the week," he laughed.

"Did it ever occur to you there will be eleven extra people at the farm and only one bathroom?"

We made quick work of closing the shop and Mr. S broke speed records getting home. Even so, by the time we pulled into the driveway, the suitcases had been unloaded, rolled sleeping bags decorated the living room floor, and boxes of groceries lined the kitchen counters. Those eleven people brought enough gear to last ten years. It occurred to me we shouldn't have bothered cleaning house. Canned sardines have more room than we did, but I didn't mind. The confusion was part of the fun.

In the dining room, Jorita was passing out paper plates and silverware like a dealer in a Las Vegas casino. Bags of chips and Fritos and cheese curls appeared along with chicken, beans, and coleslaw. Curt was digging into a cooler packed with ice and pop. "Who wants what?" he asked.

As if by magic, thirteen hungry people gravitated to the table. Even though there wasn't much elbow room, nobody minded. Laughter filled the room and everyone seemed to be talking at once, interrupting or teasing. Sometimes I carried on totally unrelated conversations with two or three people at the same time, and I loved it. Half the time, I didn't have a clue about the people they mentioned, but I laughed at the "inside" jokes anyway. They made it so natural and easy to join in.

Not long after dinner, Mr. S said he needed to take a look at the herd. Everyone but Jorita and the little kids headed toward the barn where Mr. S kept his '65 Chevy truck. Vernon and Mr. S settled into the cab. The rest of us climbed into the bed and stood holding on to the cattle racks as Mr. S pulled the truck into the north pasture and followed rutted tracks through the scrub and grass. A yellow moon and dirty headlights illuminated our way. Singing bullfrogs silenced momentarily as we passed the pond, then took up their chorus again. Waves of cricket chatter pulsed and the earthy aroma of uncut hay drifted around us. Almost as though conjured by some magician's sleight of hand, the starkly white faces of Mr. S's Herefords appeared in the darkness, sometimes so close to the truck I don't know how we missed hitting them. I could have stayed out there forever, listening to Mr. S click his tongue at the cattle and feel the wind as it carried our voices through the night.

Finally, we turned back toward the house. The little kids had been put down for the night in my room. Vernon and Jorita deposited their luggage in the bedroom at the end of the hall, and the girls and their husbands unrolled their sleeping bags in a row across the living room floor. The place looked like a disaster relief station. I almost expected to see women in Red Cross uniforms passing out coffee and sandwiches.

Mr. S watched the ten o'clock news and excused

himself with a brief, "Night, all." I couldn't believe how little his routine changed even though his house had been invaded. Maybe habits cement with age. It would probably take a lot to unsettle Mr. S for very long.

Everyone else looked ready to turn in, too, so I followed Mr. S's lead and made my way to my makeshift bed on the sleeping porch. There was enough cross ventilation to make the room comfortable, but I couldn't settle down. In the next room, I could already hear Mr. S's heavy, steady breathing. Karen, Curt, Jan, Rick, and Pam were still talking quietly in the living room. I heard Rick say something that made the rest of them hoot with laughter. Someone else warned, *shhh,* and everything was quiet again for a few minutes until another round of snickers echoed through the stillness. I sort of wished I hadn't left the room so early. I wanted to listen in and feel a part of them. God, that was frustrating. I couldn't figure out exactly where I fit in, or even *if* I fit in. Time, as they say, would tell, but that was slim consolation as I tossed and turned on my cot. The house felt full and empty, all at the same time.

Fourteen

Play Date

Rick and Jan had pulled their ski boat all the way from Iowa. Table Rock Lake, just a few miles north of the farm, is great for water sports, and the family traditionally spent Sundays taking advantage of the lake. Early morning found us loading the car with picnic baskets, coolers, blankets, and a yard darts game. Mr. S had picked out a cake with gooey yellow frosting from the bakery on Saturday, but I could've cared less. I honed in on the home-cooked goodies the family brought from Iowa. Pickles, relishes, sourdough bread, and flaky pastries were carefully stowed away with macaroni and potato salads, baked beans, and packages of shaved meats and sliced cheeses.

We were lucky to have gotten an early start, especially since the park areas are always popular on weekends. Somehow we nabbed a pavilion at the crest of a hill overlooking the lake, and we immediately staked our claim. Mr. S insisted the guys start a Jarts tournament. He *loved* playing yard darts, and during the week the family visited at the farm, he would stay out in the front yard, pitching darts in the dark. June bugs would buzz his head, but he'd keep playing, refusing to give up if a team hadn't yet reached the required twenty-one points to win.

As Mr. S paced off the length of the Jarts field, Jorita called out, "That's right, you men go right ahead and have fun. We'll unload the picnic baskets and set out the food and take care of the kids. Don't give us a second thought." Even though I thought I heard just a hint of aggravation beneath Jorita's teasing, Mr. S didn't seem bothered to leave the work to her. We spent the morning playing several games, with Rick, Curt, and I taking turns in the rotation.

When I was waiting my turn at Jarts, I spent time trying to buddy up with Bryan. Even though I had blown it with the scary eye routine the day before at the shop, he was a curious little guy, and he seemed to like the attention I showed him.

"Hey, tough guy," I said, "why don't you flex those muscles of yours?" Bryan balled his hands into tight fists and cocked his elbows, grimacing. I made a show of pinching his scrawny little arms, oohing and ahhing about his non-existent biceps. "Those are a couple of pythons you're sporting there, bud," I marveled. "If ever I need a strong man, I'm coming to find you." For the rest of the day, Bryan was all over me like a duck on a June bug. He "helped" me carry the cooler and hovered protectively by my side when I pretended to be afraid of a spider crawling across the rocks.

"I save you," he reassured me.

When it was time to eat, he grabbed my hand and pulled me to a spot beside his seat at the picnic table. He offered me bites of his carrots and helped himself to potato chips off my plate, clearly an advantageous exchange in his eyes.

By the time we finished stuffing our faces, I was itching to take a dip in the lake and try my hand at water skiing. The others seemed anxious to cool off, too, so we all changed into our suits and hot-footed it down to the swimming area.

I've never liked swimming in public pools because the water is always cloudy with chlorine. I guess they have to add a ton of the stuff to kill the germs from all the little kids who pee in the pool. Compared to the Berryville public facilities, the lake was heaven. A few little kids were splashing around in the shallow water while their mothers kept careful watch from the shore. Out by the buoys marking off the perimeter of the swimming area, an old guy floated on a neon pink air mattress.

While Rick, Jan, and Pam launched the boat, the

rest of us watched Michele show off at the edge of the water. She had just finished swimming lessons back home and had earned her official "tadpole" badge. Bryan really took to the water too, even though he was only four. He had a bucket and some small plastic bottles he filled and emptied again and again. Jorita waded in, holding Greg and Chad. She swished them around in the water until they giggled those cool baby laughs and clapped their hands.

From about a hundred yards out, Pam whistled through her teeth. Rick navigated slowly toward us, cutting the motor to idle as he neared the swimming area and allowing the momentum to carry the boat the rest of the way in. Karen and Curt and I left the kids with Mr. S, Vernon, and Jorita, and we swam the short distance to the boat. I had the option of skiing first, but I wanted to watch everyone else before making a complete fool of myself.

Karen volunteered to start on the "death board," a long piece of marine plywood about two feet wide and five feet long. A frayed yellow rope handle was the only way to hold on, which was nearly impossible until the boat picked up speed and planed out. She scooted way back on the board and gave Rick the ready sign. He throttled up and Karen squealed. In the first few seconds, she was practically invisible behind the wall of water surging over the front of the board. Once the boat reached cruising speed, the ride was a little smoother, at least until Karen started leaning hard from side to side as the board crossed the wake. Then the board would slap the water, ricochet, and nearly flip her head first into the drink.

Watching her turn a corner was the most fun. When Rick twirled his arm in a broad circle over his head, Karen covered her eyes in mock fear and screamed. In the middle of the turn, the board bounced over the wake and picked up speed.

"The 'death board' claims its bodies on the turns," Pam explained to me. "Nobody makes it all the way around, but watch Karen. She earns the most style points when she falls." True to her reputation, Karen let go of the rope, threw her legs in the air, rolled back, and cartwheeled off the board. Pam belted out an impromptu version of "Moon River," substituting "Moondoggie, wider than a mile, you're falling off in style today" for the real lyrics.

I joined in, giving my best imitation of Howard Cosell's play-by-play commentary with all his pauses and goofy inflections. "On this day, a front runner has emerged, mastering the inimitable death board with a style both fascinating and unorthodox." Karen flipped us the bird in mock anger and then laughed and slapped her palms against the surface of the water.

Curt took his turn next. Although he hadn't been on skis very often, he did all right for himself. Rick was teaching him to slalom, and it looked much harder than staying up on two skis. Jan went next. She slaloms pretty well, but Rick was the one who deserved watching. With every cut, his ski threw up a huge arc of water that looked like a shimmering roller coaster.

When it was my turn, Jan stayed beside me in the water to help me keep my balance. "Awkward" doesn't begin to describe trying to stay in an upright position with two skis sticking up out of the water. I tried to keep in a crouch with the tow rope between my legs, but my skis wouldn't cooperate. Even when I kept them parallel, the tips would slowly sink until my feet felt like dead weights hanging beneath me. Once, I got turned around so my back was to the boat. No matter what I did, I couldn't spin around the right way. If Jan hadn't been there, I would probably still be hanging in the water, my legs white and puckered and only good for fish food.

Finally, she just stayed right behind me, holding on to my life jacket to steady me until Rick gave me some power. After I got the hang of keeping myself stable, I actually did manage to pull up out of the water the first few times, but I was so surprised I either sat back down or, worse yet, fell smack on my face. One time, I completely forgot to let go of the rope. I must have swallowed ten gallons of lake water before I figured out what I was doing wrong. As I spit and sputtered, I heard Curt laughing, something about "trolling for alligators," I think.

For what it's worth, I did win the coveted "Fall of the Day" award later in the afternoon. I was finally skiing with a little bit of confidence, and I must have gotten too cocky. I pulled too much slack on the tow rope, and right away my skis shot out from under me in opposite directions. I sat down, hard, sure I was about to die. I didn't sink, though. I skidded across the water on my butt at about thirty miles an hour. When it was all over and I knew I was still among the living, I almost wished my life had ended out there. I had the worst lake water enema known to man.

"Nasty," Rick sympathized.

"Can you make it into the boat?" Karen asked.

"No problem," I gasped, but I couldn't make my legs work. Curt jumped in and pulled me back to the boat where Rick and the girls were able to grab my arms and pull me aboard. I wasn't "right" for three or four days, but at least I didn't have any regrets later in the week when the family went boating and I had to stay at the shop and work with Mr. S.

The sun and the heat and the exhaustion finally took its toll. We headed back to the farm, a quiet group, too tired to bother eating before turning in for the night.

Fifteen

Thistles

We had only one way of measuring time at the farm: Skip's Daylight Savings, which meant morning came at an ungodly hour. Out of habit, my internal clock was set to Mr. S's schedule, which usually meant hauling myself to the kitchen almost as soon as the sun was up. On this Monday, though, I slept like the dead and didn't wander in for breakfast until nearly 8:00 o'clock. The house was unusually quiet, given the extra people staying at the farm. Only Mr. S and Jorita were up. They were sitting opposite each other on the kitchen stools, drinking coffee and talking softly. The swinging door from the kitchen was closed, effectively muffling their conversation from the rest of the family who must have still been sleeping in the living room. Although subdued, their conversation seemed intense.

"...the wisest time?" Jorita was asking. "You're usually such a smart businessman, Daddy. It's unlike you to..." She looked up, saw me, and went suddenly silent.

"It isn't always about business, Jorita." Mr. S turned to me, "Morning, Ross. Why don't you join us?"

"Would you like something to eat?" Jorita offered.

"I didn't mean to interrupt," I said. "I can wait for everyone else." I turned to go, but Jorita stood and placed a hand on my arm.

"You're not interrupting a thing," she said. "Daddy and I were just talking business. He's determined to remodel the rear of the barber shop and rent it out. Mother had her own shop there when she was alive. It used to be the sweetest little place and she had it fixed up so nice, but the beauty shop has been empty since she died."

"That's been a long time, hasn't it?" I asked.

"1951. Over twenty years now," Mr. S answered.

Jorita turned back to Mr. S. "It would take a tremendous amount of work, Daddy. That part of the building hasn't been touched for so many years—not since you boarded up the entrance." There was a hint of reproach in her voice as she continued. "I'm not even sure what's left back there anymore. I know Mother's equipment is so outdated no one would want to buy it. Who knows? Maybe there's nothing left to salvage anyway." She paused, then added, almost as an afterthought, "I still think we should have sold everything years ago."

"We've been over this before, Jorita," Mr. S reminded her. "I know how you feel, and I can't say as I disagree, but I need to take care of this. Better late than never."

"Couldn't you have mentioned this earlier, before we made the trip to Berryville?" Jorita asked. "If I'd known, I would have made arrangements to stay longer than Vernon and the girls. You'll need help to sort through everything, and I'd like to be a part of that. Even after all these years, I could still use some closure. I left behind lots of memories in that shop. Anyway," she continued, "I'm just surprised, I guess, at this urgency to take care of Mother's space *now*."

Mr. S glanced at me and smiled. "Somehow young Ross here has lit a fire. I need to get my house in order."

"So you do," Jorita commented.

I had the sudden urge to be anywhere else but where I was. Mr. S and Jorita were talking about one thing, but something else was just under the surface, and I had the distinct feeling there was more to their exchange than differences about real estate.

Just then Pam walked in, holding Greg. "The twins are up, and everyone else is stirring. What's for breakfast?"

"I thought I'd start with Daddy's favorite," Jorita answered. "Biscuits and gravy. Why don't you set the table and rouse the others. I could use some help."

"Right. I'm on it," Pam said. She held Greg out toward me. I took him and cradled him in the crook of my arm. "Careful, he's wet," Pam cautioned. In nothing flat, I stretched Greg out away from me at arm's length. Everyone hooted.

"Ever change a diaper?" she asked. I shook my head no, and she laughed. "Better learn to pull your weight, then. Why don't you take him back in the living room and ask Jan for a lesson. I'll expect a full report. Oh, and by the way, pray there's no poop. Greg's dumps are legend." She laughed in dismissal and turned to the cabinets.

I escaped to the living room and found Jan, who took pity on me. She whisked Greg away to the middle bedroom and did her thing while I helped roll up the sleeping bags and stacked them behind the couch.

All the time I was straightening the room, I stewed about Mr. S's comment. He said he needed to get his house in order, and he implied I was the reason behind his decision. It was like he and I had neatly worked out a grand plan for the beauty shop and Jorita wasn't even part of the equation. Heck, he'd never even *mentioned* the old beauty shop to me. Sure, I'd seen the outside entrance and the painted mural, and I knew Mr. S's shop had at one time connected to the rear part of the building, but he had never said anything about his wife's beauty shop being housed there. That place meant nothing to me. Still, I felt like I wanted to apologize to Jorita, but I wasn't quite sure for what.

When I went back into the kitchen a few minutes later, though, I convinced myself I was imagining things. Jorita was happily directing preparations for breakfast. While she fried sausage patties in the iron skillet, Jan was cleaning and slicing strawberries and melon, Karen was cracking eggs into a bowl, and Pam was stirring a big pot of creamy gravy.

Breakfast was served at the dining table, and we were like opposing generals grouped around a battlefield map. Reaching for the last sausage patty was as tough as taking a hill from enemy combatants. If you claimed a biscuit without being stabbed in the back of the hand by someone else's fork, you won the war.

The confusion and conversation only quieted near the end of the meal. Karen, who was sitting next to me, nudged me with her elbow and nodded toward Mr. S. He sat nearly motionless, his eyes focused on his youngest granddaughter, his fingers laced together and resting on his belly. He was listening to Pam recount some story about a food fight at Hillcrest, the dining hall for her dorm at the University of Iowa. Although the story wasn't all that thrilling, he seemed entranced.

"He can't believe *anyone* can talk that fast for that

long," Karen explained in a stage whisper. "She's a phenom. Look. He just watches her mouth move."

"I heard that," Pam advised. "Jealous? You only *wish* you could be this fascinating."

At that, Mr. S threw his head back and laughed. "I believe I'll go wash out my teeth," he said, "and then maybe you and I can go to town, Jorita. We'll look at your mother's shop together and then we can decide what to do about Faye's things."

Jorita agreed immediately and began clearing the table. Even though Mr. S had initially pinned this little venture on me, I was glad he hadn't invited me to join them, and I guessed Jorita was glad, too.

They left not long after. I suggested we might try throwing a line in the pond or maybe a few of us could ride horses, but the family looked at me as though I'd just proposed we go wading in alligator-infested waters.

"I don't think so," Jan said.

"Why not?" I asked.

"Today is Monday," Vernon explained.

"Yeah. Monday. Almost always follows Sunday. I've got it," I answered. "Clear skies, hot weather, a day off from work at the shop."

"At the shop, maybe. Not on the farm. Mondays are for milk thistles," Vernon insisted. "Whether Skip is here on not, we cut thistles on Monday."

"Ever since I married into this family," Rick

interjected, "we've been cutting thistles. Usually Skip is with us, but even when he has something else to do, we know the routine. We should. We've been doing it for years."

"I've been here for two months and I've NEVER cut thistles...not on Monday or any other day," I said. "Don't the cows eat them? They seem to graze on everything else."

"Too thorny," Vernon said. "The cows avoid them like the plague. If we don't control them, they spread like a nasty rumor."

"Have you ever heard of weed killers?" I asked sarcastically.

"You're looking at 'em," Vernon said. "Skip doesn't believe in poisoning the ground with chemicals, so we cut the thistles."

"Skip's no dummy," Curt explained. "We're an army of cheap labor. We can cover lots of ground in one day, and we have the drill down pat. Come on. It's not so bad. We'll initiate you."

And so I found myself seated on the dropped tailgate of the 65 Chevy with hoe in gloved hands. Everyone but Jan had been pressed into service. She stayed back to take care of the twins, usually Jorita's responsibility on thistle days, but even Bryan was along for the ride. "I'm cut sissles, too," he announced with pride.

Vernon took over Mr. S's usual job—driving the

truck. I guessed there was at least one advantage to being the oldest guy in the group, because Vernon didn't seem to mind his assignment at all. Rick and Curt took turns hopping down to open and shut the gates as we drove from pasture to pasture and then Vernon would methodically zigzag across the fields, stopping whenever anyone yelled "WEED."

Like warriors fueled by blood lust, we descended on the thistles, usually knee-high or taller and deceptively pretty with their purple flowers. We hacked with our hoes at the spiky plants, carefully avoiding their razor sharp leaves as we tossed the uprooted remains into the back of the pick-up. By the end of the day, we had obliterated a mountain of thistles. Rick made a competition of the work, tallying our weed whacking efforts into statistics of success he measured by the size of the blisters on our palms. Bryan and I, the two rookies, competed for "Thistle Killer of the Year," and by a unanimous show of hands, he was declared the winner. He gave me a high five and strutted toward the truck, all smiles.

"Just one last job before we're done," Vernon said. He drove to a ditch running through the north pasture, where we pitch-forked the weeds into an impressive pile. "Once these dry out, I'll bet Skip will have you on burn duty," Rick predicted.

"I think you should claim a trophy before that happens," Pam said. She retrieved one of the larger thistles from the pile, carefully stripping away the prickly leaves but preserving the tufted purple blossom. "Now Granddad will know you're officially thistle-worthy. We should pin it to your tee shirt when we go home."

"Just don't let Granddad talk you into tasting the milky stuff from the thistle stems," Karen advised. "He's a big one for natural cures, and he read someplace thistle juice is good for the liver."

"Yep," Pam joked. "A little knowledge is a dangerous thing for an unsuspecting guinea pig, especially if you're the guinea pig."

"Remember his remedy for farting?" Karen laughed. "I think he mixed spice—maybe ground ginger—with asafetida, rock salt and warm water."

"I don't even want to know what *asafetida* is," I said.

"Then don't drop a bomb," Pam said, "at least not in front of Granddad."

"I'll do my best," I promised. "What's the cure for a growling stomach?"

"Don't worry, that's easy to fix," Vernon said. "If I know Jorita, she'll have a feast ready the minute we walk in the door. Let's head back."

A hot meal of fried chicken and mashed potatoes was waiting for us. Jorita was just dishing up some steaming green beans and Jan was slicing juicy red tomatoes. Although we all badly needed showers, we settled for scouring our hands and splashing water on our faces before sitting down to supper.

The table had been decorated with a vase of freshly-cut field daisies. "I found this vase back in Mother's shop," Jorita said. "Remember, Daddy, how the crystal pieces were her favorites? When I couldn't find this particular vase in the house after she died, I'd just assumed it had been broken. But look. Not a chip anywhere." The sharp edges of the tall, slender vase caught the light from the fixture over the table, throwing a rainbow of colors onto the white tablecloth.

"Flowers?" Vernon said. "What's the occasion? Did I forget an anniversary?"

"They're to celebrate a partnership," Jorita explained. "Mother's vase, daisies from Daddy's ditch, and my special talent for organizing."

Mr. S elaborated. "Jorita and I hashed over some plans for the shop. We *are* going to remodel, but not right away. After the weather turns a bit cooler, she promised to come down for as long as I need her and we'll do what's necessary."

"The place is absolute chaos," Jorita said, almost happily. "Daddy couldn't begin to sort through it by himself. We'll have our work cut out for us."

If anyone wondered where *I'd* be during this massive operation, they didn't let on. And then, smooth as silk, Jorita added, "Of course, Ross will be able to help, too."

"Of course," I echoed, but an uncomfortable silence followed.

"Announcement! Announcement!" Karen interjected. "In case you've forgotten, Granddad, today was Milk Thistle Monday, and Ross has become an official weed whacker of the first order. We present you with a symbol of his accomplishment." She nodded to Pam, who produced the thistle blossom, now slightly bedraggled, and presented it with a flourish to Mr. S.

"Well done, young man," he said. "You were taught by the best. And, of course, they were taught by the best, too." Mr. S grinned and made a big show of sticking the purple thistle in among the snowy white daisies.

As the rest of the family looked on, I felt an unreasonable swell of pride. It's silly, I know, but nobody could deny it—in a bouquet of delicate flowers, that noxious weed looked right at home.

Sixteen

The Child Within

Mr. S had lived seventy-five years without ever having an honest-to-goodness, cake and ice cream, balloon and streamers birthday party. I could hardly believe that. I mean, The Cedars wasn't a prison or anything. The teachers and counselors tried to make a big deal over birthdays. While it wasn't cool to act like you enjoyed the fuss, every single one of us would have been disappointed if his birthday had gone by unnoticed.

From the sounds of their plans, Jorita and the family were going all out to make this celebration a special one for Mr. S. The big day was Thursday, August 7. Jorita had found a bright red, short sleeved one-piece work suit. She had sewn wide bands of white and blue sequins around the neck and sleeves of the suit and fastened a big blue tassel to the zipper in the front. Pam had carefully painted a Superman-shaped "S" in acrylics on a matching piece of red cotton and attached it to the back of the suit. The package was wrapped in metallic gold and silver paper topped by an enormous gold bow. All the attached cards were addressed to "Super Dad," "Super Granddad," and "Super Papa."

The family had also gotten a decorative, miniature windmill to put in his front yard and a rustic, custom-made wooden sign that said "Skip's Barber Shop." An artist friend of Karen's had done the hand lettering, and it was really classy. I knew Mr. S would love the windmill and the sign. I wasn't too sure about the red suit, though. Jorita had enough foresight to just baste the sequins on so he could take them off after everybody had a good laugh.

The biggest problem was pulling off a surprise party. The family had schemed long and hard back in Iowa, and they mapped out a great plan. Generously, they included me in their preparations.

On Wednesday night, after Mr. S had watched the news and gone to bed, Jorita tiptoed into his room. Careful not to disturb him, she silently lifted the keys to the shop from the top of his bureau. Without a word, Curt, Karen, Rick, Jan, Pam, and I crept out to Curt's Monterey. Karen slid behind the wheel and shifted into neutral. She signaled for us guys to push the car out onto the highway. The crunching gravel beneath the tires sounded like machine-gun fire to us, but even Geraldine took no notice. Although Mr. S's bedroom light didn't come on, we didn't risk turning on the car's headlights or starting the engine until we had coasted several hundred feet down the highway. When we were safely out of earshot, Curt took the wheel and the rest of us piled into the car.

Berryville resembled a ghost town—not a soul on the sidewalks, not a single car in the square. Curt pulled the car into a parking space in front of the Mercantile right across from the shop, and Karen hit the light switch as soon as we opened the doors. With that glass front along the street, we were lit up like motorized window mannequins during Christmas season.

Pam had packed an enormous roll of double-wide butcher paper and some brightly colored Magic Markers. The girls headed for the back room, unrolled the paper, and began making a huge banner proclaiming "Happy 75th Birthday, Granddad!" While they were busy being artistic, Curt and Rick and I decorated the room with balloons and crepe paper streamers. Starting at each of the four corners of the room, we twisted the crepe paper into spirals and tried to tape the ends in place. We had forgotten to bring the ladder from the garage, though, and there was no way to reach those high ceilings without something to stand on. Rick suggested we move a table in from the back room and put a chair on top of that. Curt was the tallest, and he could probably reach the ceiling that way. While I waited in the shop, leaning against the table that held the cash register, Rick and Curt disappeared into the back room.

"Haven't changed much, have you, punk?" I whirled around to see Sheriff Stoner standing just inside the double doors. His right hand rested at his belt. The other was clenched tightly. Just outside, I could see his patrol car, lights out, pulled up over the curb onto the sidewalk.

"What in the hell are you doing here after hours?" Stoner demanded. "You planning to take some money from the cash box? Gonna deface Mr. Skipworth's property like you did the fountain?" He shook his head. "This'll just break him. It's gonna tear him apart." He paused, then asked, "How'd you get yourself out here, anyway? Whose car is outside? Someone from The Cedars here to help?"

"Hey, guys," I called. "You better get out here. The sheriff's on to us." I could barely keep from laughing right in Stoner's face. He must have thought he was Barney Fife or something.

Curt and Rick came through the curtained doorway carrying a heavy table. They had taken a lot of time clearing off Mr. S's junk, but their timing couldn't have been more perfect. Stoner's eyes almost popped out of his head. He probably thought he had cracked a major crime ring.

"Brought some friends, did you?" growled Stoner. "No problem. I've got plenty of room for the lot of you." He stared holes through Curt and Rick before sneering back at me. "You running with older scum now, boy?"

That was all I could take. I plopped down in Mr. S's barber chair, threw back my head, and laughed 'til I was nearly sick. The other guys looked at Stoner as though he had just escaped from a mental institution. All the noise brought Karen, Jan, and Pam into the room, an entrance which probably pushed Stoner's blood pressure off the meter.

"What—in—the—hell?" Stoner howled.

I made the formal introductions. Stoner turned four shades of green when he found out my fellow "scum" were Mr. S's grandkids.

Stoner kind of stuttered and shuffled around. You could tell he was praying for an earthquake to open a hole right under his feet. He made his retreat, backing out of the room like a cornered animal. He was so apologetic, in fact, I almost felt sorry for him.

"...perfectly understandable mistake," he mumbled. "Sorry as I can be."

He vanished like dew in the morning sun. We all had a good laugh then, and I knew Mr. S would get a kick out of the story. Just anticipating his reaction was as good as any party for me.

The room looked terrific when we finally finished.

The butcher paper sign stretched all along the back wall of the shop, completely covering the mirror. Streamers had been taped from each corner to the center light, making the room look like the inside of a circus tent. We had tied bunches of balloons from each slat in the ceiling fan, and other balloons were tied to the shoeshine stand and coat rack. We had even wrapped crepe paper around the armrests and pedestal of Mr. S's barber chair. Every customer could pick up a frosted cupcake and celebrate right along with us. In a small town like Berryville, everybody and his brother would know about Mr. S's birthday before the end of the day.

Surprising Mr. S was as important as the decorations. Since Jorita woke up at the crack of dawn anyway, she was going to sneak into the living room on Thursday morning and wake everyone. The family planned to get dressed and slip back into their sleeping bags before Mr. S woke up. I was supposed to go into town with him like always, but I had to delay him from opening the shop for about fifteen minutes. That way, the family could leave after we did and still arrive at the shop before us.

Every plan I concocted to keep Mr. S from the shop sounded dopey to me. I knew he'd see right through me if I made up some lie, so I eventually settled on a half-truth that sounded reasonable. As Jorita (a bathrobe over her dress), Mr. S, and I stood in the kitchen, I told Mr. S I had found his scrapbook the night before. I told him I read about Old Bill, his farm hand, and I told him on our way into town I wanted to stop by the cemetery where Bill was buried. Mr. S wasn't particularly enthusiastic about the idea until Jorita saved the show by offering to go with us.

"I always visit Mother's grave, Daddy," she said. "Why don't we go together this year? There are things I can do in town until Vernon can pick me up." Mr. S couldn't refuse us both, so Jorita left the kitchen to "change" and tell Vernon about the new plan. In a few minutes, we were on our way to the cemetery, barely a mile down the highway toward town. I knew as soon as our car hit the highway, the rest of the family would be whipping around like a Kansas twister. They would kick sleeping bags in a corner and collect the cupcakes and kids and cameras.

Mr. S pulled the Chevy into the circular gravel road in front of Farmer's Cemetery. The three of us walked slowly up the incline leading through the wrought iron arch. Unpolished markers fixed with rusted plates bearing names and dates were scattered throughout the cemetery. Sun-bleached plastic flowers decorated some of the headstones, which made them seem sadder, somehow. Other graves were so overgrown with weeds the markers were hard to read.

The Skipworth plot was marked by a brick-colored marble headstone with the family name engraved

across the top. Below that, in smaller letters, was
    FAYE 1909—1951   LUTHER 1900—
"Old Bill" Dimmick's grave sat just to the left, the headstone identical to the Skipworth's, only smaller. The whole thing was incredibly depressing, and I stayed at the gravesite only long enough to keep Mr. S from getting suspicious.

I wandered over to the edge of the cemetery nearest the highway and watched for the family to pass by on their way into town. They must have made record time because we had only been at the graveyard for six or seven minutes before I saw Curt's Monterey and Rick's Monte Carlo whiz by. I had done my job, and I wanted to leave as soon as possible. Something about Mr. S's having a triple-wide plot marked out when there were only two occupants made me uneasy. I walked back to the grave, anxious to be away.

Jorita and Mr. S had been standing together, talking quietly. I think Jorita had almost forgotten we were there only to delay Mr. S for a few minutes.

"We lost her when she was so young," she said, but she seemed to be talking as much to herself as to me or Mr. S. "Has Daddy ever told you the story?" I shook my head.

"Vernon and I were stationed at Fort Collins in Colorado, and Mother was visiting us on the base while she recovered from abdominal surgery. Daddy had stayed home to work at the shop and run the farm.

Mother developed complications, peritonitis, and she was so sick from the infection. We called Daddy to tell him Mother was dying and he needed to hurry, but the closest place to catch a flight was in Kansas City. He started driving, but the Kansas State Troopers intercepted him before he reached the airport. Mother was already gone."

She paused before continuing. "Daddy made the flight to Colorado and then we had to deal with so many arrangements to bring her body home to Berryville. It was pure hell." Mr. S had once told me he didn't like to fly. Now I understood why.

Tears welled in the corners of her eyes, and I wondered if the pain of losing someone you love ever gets any easier. Almost as if she read my mind, she self- consciously swiped at her tears.

"Even after all these years, I still miss Mother," she acknowledged. "And being here is just... well, it's hard." She choked back a little sob and blew her nose. She took a deep, settling breath and wrapped her arms around herself. "Back home, Reverend Buchanan would say tears are midwives that give birth to sorrow and usher in grief. If we allow ourselves to grieve, we are open to grace."

Mr. Skipworth made a little contemptuous sucking sound.

"Do you really believe that?" I asked.

"I believe joy is the other side of sorrow, just as life

is the other side of death." She glanced sideways at Mr. S. "Simplistic, maybe, but comforting, just the same."

"We should probably get going," Mr. S suggested. "I need to open the shop."

Jorita took a few minutes, but she finally turned and made her way back to the car. Silence marked the rest of the ride to town, hardly a party atmosphere.

Cameras loaded and ready, the family had stationed themselves in the shop directly across from the double doors. When Mr. S walked in, everyone yelled "SURPRISE!" and "HAPPY BIRTHDAY!" He stood absolutely still, mouth hanging open, trying to let everything register at once. When he was able to speak at last, all he could manage was, "My word. My word." The rest of us were beaming like we'd just won the lottery. Michele escorted Mr. S to his chair and presented his gifts to him.

I got a real kick watching him open his presents. Everything had to be methodically inspected, piece-by-piece, before he could move on to the next package. I thought he was going to make us assemble the windmill right there in the shop. Mr. S oohed and ahhed over the sign, too. He even refused to open the last package until everyone had a hand in hanging the sign at just the right spot in the shop's front window. Then, of course, we had to take pictures of Mr. S standing beside the sign.

Finally, Michele produced the box with the sequined Superman suit. At first, Mr. S thought he'd been given just another pair of coveralls. Then he lifted the red suit from the box, noticing the shiny sequins and the showy "Super Skip" patch on the back. "I can't wear this on the farm," he joked. "I'll spook the cattle."

"You have to promise to model it for us when we get back to the farm," Karen said.

"That's a dandy," was all Mr. S would say.

About nine, the family trooped down to the Ozark Café for breakfast. Afterwards, they returned to the shop for a few minutes before driving back out to the farm. Jorita was planning a feast for Mr. S's birthday dinner, and she needed the better part of the day to prepare. The guys talked about running some errands and doing a few odd jobs around the farm so we could all spend an uninterrupted evening together.

Even though the family had gone, every customer or passerby who wandered in kept the day-long party alive. Mr. S explained to each new arrival how we crept into town to decorate the shop. Then he described his presents down to the last detail. He finally hung the red suit on the coat rack so everyone could admire the workmanship.

At home that night, Mr. S tried on the Superman suit and struck a few funny poses for the family. In one of the shots, he held each end of a curved metal rod, his face twisted in a grimace as though he had just bent steel with his bare hands. For another picture, he took the stance of a body builder with arms flexed and one knee cocked. He was a real ham, modeling his coveralls. And the funny part is, even though I never saw him wear the suit again, he wouldn't let Jorita remove the tassel or sequins or Superman patch.

Just before bedtime, Michele brought out her Mattel Creepy Crawlers set. "Help me, Papa. Help me make a bug."

I had seen Creepy Crawlers advertised on television, and I could see how they'd appeal to little kids. The set had a low-wattage heating chamber and molds in the shape of different critters like lizards and beetles and worms. When "magic" liquid was poured into the molds and heated, gummy-textured Crawlers materialized. Once the squiggly bugs cooled, kids could decorate them with special paints.

As the rest of the family huddled around Mr. S and Michele, offering advice on the best color of goo for each of the Crawlers, Jorita and I stood aside. "Sometimes, I swear, Daddy's like a kid himself," she said. Then she recounted the way Mr. S's mother had died when he was only ten years old, and how he was shuffled around to different relatives until he was old enough to fend for himself. "He was always a little shorter than other boys, but he didn't ever back down from a challenge," she noted with a chuckle. "Daddy used to tell me he needed to be tough, and he took pride that he survived the loss of his mother." Then she motioned to Mr. S and Michele. "But I don't think he ever survived the loss of his childhood. Look at him."

Mr. S, decked out in his Superman suit, lay on his belly alongside his great-granddaughter. There, propped on his elbows, he carefully painted his Creepy Crawler with the single-minded concentration of the child he never had the chance to be.

Seventeen

Subtraction and Long Division

Friday, the family's last night at the farm, we all gathered around the dining room table. Curt and Rick and Vernon were busy painting the tips of the windmill bright red because Mr. S thought his gift needed a little flash. Then, just as always, Mr. S left us to watch the news and go to bed.

Pam mentioned how hard it was to leave after such a good week, and then Karen turned to me. "I'm glad Granddad has you around, Ross," she said. "Sometimes I worry about him out here on the farm all by himself."

Suddenly, Jorita stood up and left the room, mumbling something about some last minute packing. Vernon waited only a minute before he followed her. I heard the door close behind them. A stiff, uncomfortable silence accompanied their quick exits.

Pam, always the one to name the obvious, cleared her throat. "Okay, then. That can't be good." She looked around the table and added, "Just because they left doesn't mean we have to act like this is a funeral."

"What do you think is wrong?" Karen wondered. "Mom looked like she was about to cry. Maybe I should go see if I can help."

"No," Jan disagreed. "Dad's in there with her. If she wants to tell us, we'll find out soon enough."

We didn't find out. I did. After a few minutes, I excused myself from the group under the pretense of going to the john. I made a point of closing the bathroom door before creeping down the hallway, wincing when the boards around the floor furnace grate creaked beneath my weight. I stood motionless, my eyes squeezed tightly shut, hoping Vernon and Jorita had not heard me. Their muffled voices continued without a break, so I tiptoed down the remaining stretch of hallway. I leaned against the wall in the corner by their door and strained to hear their quiet conversation. Not the proudest moment of my life, I admit, but I couldn't help myself.

Jorita was crying, softly. "I can't do this anymore, Vernon. I can't. From the beginning, I've been worried. When Daddy first told me about Ross, I'd never in a million years have believed it would get to this point."

"Hon, I know," Vernon responded. "I don't think

any of us expected an adoption hearing would ever reach a judge. But think about this. Maybe it'll be a relief Ross will be here to help look out for Skip."

"It's not that and you know it," Jorita said.

Then what is it? I wanted to shout.

"Don't do this to yourself, Jo," Vernon insisted.

My mind spun in confusion. Why did she dislike me so? Why had she kept her objections to herself? I didn't listen anymore. I didn't want to hear.

Betrayal is an ugly word. Even when Major set Sheriff Stoner on my back that Saturday in June (it seemed like ages ago), I had not felt as hurt and angry as I did that night. Without even caring if Jorita and Vernon heard me, I ran down the hall, through the living room, and out the front door. On my way past the dining room I saw the rest of the family look up, their faces frozen in surprise. They probably felt the same way Jorita did, and—like her—they had been silent. I didn't care. I didn't care if they all packed up and left right then, right on the spot. In fact, I hoped I'd never have to lay eyes on any of them again.

I ran to the barn, drawn to the loft. In the dark, I felt my way up the ladder and threw myself down on a bale of hay. Outside, I could hear my name called over and over.

Screw you all, I thought.

Finally, Rick said, "Let's give this up. It's obvious

he doesn't want us to find him."

"Why did he run out like that?" Pam asked.

"I think I know why," Jorita answered. I could hear her telling them bits of what I had just overheard. Her voice kept getting softer, fading as the family walked back toward the house. Soothing night sounds—crickets and wind and cattle—filled the silence, but I didn't fall asleep for a long, long time.

Eighteen

Love Letter

Call me a stupid coward, but I stayed in the barn until I was sure Mr. S had left for the shop and the family had loaded the cars and headed back north. I didn't really want this to be my last memory of them, but that was the choice I made.

They were a quiet group that morning. Through a gap in the boards of the barn I could hear them making trip after trip between the house and their cars. I watched them as they moved like reluctant robots, mindlessly performing pre-assigned tasks.

Jorita's eyes were red and swollen. She kept asking everyone to try and find me before they left. When they couldn't delay any longer, she almost collapsed.

"If I could only see him before we go," she cried, "maybe I could make him understand."

"Give it up, Mom," Karen advised. "Nothing you

could say will change anything. He'll hear what he wants to hear."

"It'll be okay. You'll see," Rick comforted.

With one final look around, Jorita allowed herself to be coaxed into the car. As the family finally drove away, I held back my own tears.

I'd have a lot of explaining to do when Mr. S came home from the shop. To keep busy, I started to move my gear from the sleeping porch back into my old room. The sheets on the bed had been freshly made. The corners of the bedspread had been meticulously tucked in, something I never bothered to do. On my gleaming dresser, a small white envelope was propped against the mirror. I sat on the bed for a long time before I mustered enough courage to read the note inside. It was from Jorita, as I knew it would be.

> *Ross,*
>
> *This is such a poor substitute for speaking to you in person I hesitate to even write this note. My only hope is you will read it and try to understand.*
>
> *After you ran out last night, I guessed you had overheard some of my conversation with Vernon. For that, I am so very sorry. I was not honest with you, and that is unforgivable. I have tried to talk to Daddy these past few weeks, but he didn't want to*

listen…a dance we have rehearsed over and over through the years. Please understand, Ross, my objections to this proposed adoption are not personally directed at you. I suppose it's too late to try and explain why I was silent, but given the difference in your ages, no one could have convinced me this adoption would be allowed to proceed. I was content to let the court bear the brunt of killing the petition. That didn't happen, and so here we are.

I am concerned for him. I don't want him to be hurt. And whether you believe it possible or not, you will hurt him. You won't intend to, but you will. It won't be because you don't care for Daddy, though. You will hurt him because you will not always be a young man who needs his help. Daddy's world is shrinking. Yours is expanding. You will hurt him because he will need you more than you need him. Despite what any court might decree, his need is not your responsibility, and he cannot understand that.

I told Daddy everything I am telling you now. We talked well into the morning. He heard what I had to say, but he disagrees with me. I have to respect his wishes, but at least I have cleared my conscience with him. For that, I feel some measure of relief. My only regret is I must leave without telling you my feelings to your face. I apologize for not leveling with you earlier.

Perhaps I look for trouble where none exists. I passionately hope that is the case, for never in my life have I so wanted to be wrong.

Please understand.
Jorita

Well, she was wrong, and I was determined to prove it. She didn't know what was going to happen. No one can predict the future.

Nineteen

Regroup

Mr. S must have had some late customers, because he didn't get home until after six. He looked awfully tired when he walked into the kitchen. I remember thinking he looked old.

"So, you decided to show yourself, did you?" he asked.

I was immediately on the defensive. "I couldn't help it. I didn't want to see Jorita. She made me feel like I was a part of her family, but she lied."

"*Lied* is a pretty strong word, Ross. And if you wanted to make Jorita suffer, you succeeded. She's crushed. She's been harder on herself than she deserves." His eyes were hard and unforgiving. "She told me what happened last night, and I don't blame you for being angry. I had words with her myself on that score. But Jorita is concerned because she cares about us." He emphasized *us*. "She didn't think she'd ever have to voice her doubts because she figured the adoption would never make it past the hearing." Mr. S paused. "If she didn't care, son, she wouldn't have given either of us a second thought."

"By keeping quiet, she's hurt both of us," I accused. "How does that show she cares?"

"Does your reaction erase the hurt? Does your anger make everything right? Do you feel better?" His tone was brutal.

Refusing to back down, I said the first thing I could think of. "She was wrong. She doesn't deserve my forgiveness… or yours."

He looked at me squarely and set his jaw as if to keep himself from speaking out in anger. When he did speak, his voice was almost a whisper, but he emphasized every word.

"Perhaps the same thing could have been said about you back in June. Then you would never have suffered this injustice, Ross."

He was right and I knew it, but my pride would not allow me to admit it. I clenched my teeth and fixed my gaze on the wall behind him.

"I see the subject is closed," Mr. S said. "Very well, but make sure you never speak of this to me again." He turned toward his room to change into his work clothes. "If you're not too busy feeling sorry for yourself, maybe we could have some supper. It's been a long day."

The evening was long and quiet. Each of us did our best to avoid the other one. If we happened to pass in the doorway, we made exaggerated detours around one another as though any physical contact would be like contracting leprosy. To top it off, the house felt like an empty mausoleum. There was no family to make noise and laugh and chase around. Voices from the TV echoed in the stillness.

We never again talked about the tension between Jorita and me. Gradually, as the routine of our lives settled back into a familiar pattern, the scene became little more than a bad memory. Jorita still wrote or called every week, and she and Mr. S had no problems finding things to talk about. If I happened to answer one of her long-distance phone calls, I spoke only until I could get Mr. S on the line. I would say a quick, cold goodbye and go off by myself for awhile. I *acted* hurt and unhappy long after I *felt* hurt and unhappy, and it bothered me. After playing the victim for so long, I didn't quite know how to shed the role. Instead of talking to Jorita and clearing the air with her, I clammed up and tried to feel sorry for myself. Then I forgot about my pretended anger until the next time I had to talk to her.

Really, there wasn't much to interrupt our lives in the few weeks before school started. In fact, August seemed to drag on until I was sure it must be Thanksgiving. With help from Sara, I registered for my fall term at High. I got every class I wanted except Popular Literature. There was a conflict between that and Intro to Chemistry. Since I already had another lit course, I decided to get the science requirement out of the way. The only trouble was Mr. Flory taught the class and, according to Sara, couldn't be pleased unless you were another Einstein or something. She told me not to worry, though, even if I did have trouble. There would probably be some repeat juniors and seniors in the class with lots of experience. Mr. Flory was an institution at High. If you had him and didn't flunk, you just didn't have any status.

Sara laughed at me when I insisted on buying my supplies before Sophomore Orientation Day. Ignoring her good-natured suggestion I purchase kindergarten-sized crayons and a pencil with an owl-shaped eraser, I stocked up on spiral note pads and folders for every subject. I probably did act like a kid just starting first grade, but I didn't care. The Cedars had never given me much reason to get excited about school. I planned to enjoy the anticipation for as long as I could.

The prospect of football was another bright spot. I had a chance to meet the coach one day in the shop. I didn't realize who he was until Mr. S (who never watched a sporting event on TV or in person as long as I knew him) began talking to the coach about the upcoming season.

Coach Rothrock, "Rocky" to his players, needed

only one or two questions before he started talking about new offensive formations and defensive strategy and returning lettermen. While Mr. S gave Coach the buzz he asked for, Rocky talked as if we were in the locker room at halftime and Green Forest was beating High 21-0. When I timidly expressed some interest in coming out for the team, Rocky—looking more and more like a drill sergeant in the Marines—gave me the once over.

"Fair set of shoulders on you, but you're kinda puny. I've seen meatier wings and thighs on my momma's fried chicken," he noted. "Ever lift weights?"

"No, sir, I..."

"Oughta start. Never too late to work out," Rocky advised. "Might help you earn a position on the squad. Can you run? You're too small for the line. Ya'd get killed."

I decided Coach didn't expect an answer to his questions, so I quit trying to talk. Instead, I sat back and listened, trying not to laugh at Mr. S who was trying not to laugh at me. When Rocky left, satisfied he was only a little hairier than a cue ball, Mr. S grinned broadly and winked at me.

"Now there's a man who likes the sound of his own voice."

In a way, I felt like time had been thrown in reverse, right back to the first day I worked for Mr. S.

Then, like now, he made some funny remark about his customers that helped to ease the tension between us. We hadn't really talked for a long time, much less laughed together. It felt pretty good, believe me.

We talked about Rocky, about football, about school, about my schedule, about me. Mr. S told me I was lucky to get a chance to earn a diploma because no one could take an education away from me. People at The Cedars had been preaching that same thing for years, but they never carried the weight that Mr. S did. He never had more than a third grade education, and he had to fight to learn on his own.

"Make the most of every opportunity, Ross," Mr. S said solemnly. "Read everything you can, study hard, and be curious about the world your whole life."

I got to thinking about how different our lives would be once school started. I'd only be able to work at the shop on Saturdays. I wouldn't be home on Mondays with Mr. S, and I'd probably be busy every day after school. I suppose that's why I suggested the trip.

Mr. S had talked a little about his childhood, but most of what I knew came from conversations I had with Jorita. His past was kind of like a mystery to me. I figured if we took a weekend trip back to his birthplace in Missouri, we could spend some time together before my school schedule got too busy, and I would get to know a little more about Mr. S at the same time.

He was reluctant when I first suggested we take off on the upcoming Labor Day weekend, the last weekend before school. He couldn't remember ever closing the shop on a Saturday unless it was a life-and-death emergency. That was probably the toughest obstacle to hurdle. Once I convinced him to take his own advice and "make the most of every opportunity," he came up with the excuse he was too old to drive that far. I countered with the fact I had earned my learner's permit at The Cedars, and I wouldn't mind doing most of the driving anyway. Besides, Many Springs looked like about a two-hundred mile trip, only half a day's drive.

Surprisingly, Mr. S agreed. We spent the rest of the afternoon with Arkansas and Missouri road maps, planning our route. As it turned out, we didn't have a whole lot of choice. The highways in the Ozarks don't do much more than snake their way from one little town to another, but it was still fun to mark our road with a red pen. I made a mental note of the towns we'd pass through: Yellville, Cotter, Mountain Home, Viola.

We planned on leaving Berryville about seven or eight on Saturday morning, take our time, and still be in Many Springs by lunchtime. Mr. S wasn't sure what the town was like now, or if there would be anyplace nearby to get something to eat and spend the night. Thinking ahead, we packed a huge lunch and filled a thermos with iced tea. We stopped at the bakery on our way home from town Friday night and practically bought out the place. We got enough doughnuts for breakfast, desserts, and snacks along the way.

The countryside was beautiful that Saturday morning. We managed to start even earlier than we had planned, and the sun was just rising behind the mountains when we pulled out of the drive. A rosy golden mist at the horizon deepened into a purple velvet sky. Low-lying valleys cradled cottony fog that shrouded our view of the road ahead. Everything was still and quiet, and Mr. S and I shared a peace we hadn't enjoyed in a long time.

Mr. S. drove first. As the miles rolled away beneath us, he began to talk about things he remembered as a little boy. We were drawn to his home place like metal to a magnet. The closer we came to Many Springs, the more freely his words flowed. He told me himself about his mother's death, and about how frightened and lost he felt for a long time afterwards. He recalled the kindness of friends and relatives who took him in for short periods, but he didn't ever feel really attached to any of them. He said until the last few years of his life, he had trouble showing any physical affection for his family.

"I know there were times when Jorita was a little girl she'd want to sit on my lap or put her arms around my neck," he remembered. "I would always put her off because I didn't feel very comfortable about it. Nobody held me much after my mother died. I had just turned ten, and I guess I was supposed to accept her death like a man."

"But you do okay with your grandkids," I observed. "Michele always wants to hug you, and you hold Bryan and the twins all the time. The girls make a big deal out of kissing you on your head," I laughed.

Mr. S smiled. "Yep," he admitted. "Guess I don't mind so much after all."

As Mr. S talked about himself, I began to realize just how little I really knew about him—much less than he knew about me, in fact. His stories about being a carnival barker, an official witness at a hanging, and a volunteer firefighter who had seen people suffer the most horrible kind of death seemed like pieces of a jigsaw puzzle. He had seen and done and probably forgotten more things than I could ever imagine, but each of his recollections added another puzzle piece. Someday, he might reveal a complete picture of himself. I kept wondering if, once I got to be as old as Mr. S, I'd have the same kind of long-forgotten stories to tell someone. But then, I'm always doing that. I put myself in some dream situation and try to imagine how I'd act and what I'd do. It's like I have a closed-circuit video system in my head. Once I tune in on my private screen, I'm in another world.

I must have been in my trance for a while, because

Mr. S said something about "in one ear and out the other." It took a couple of minutes to realize he was talking to me.

Out of the blue, I asked, "Why did you take me in, Mr. S?"

"Well, now. What's got you thinking about that so suddenly? Seems like a funny time to be asking that question."

Maybe so, I thought. *Or maybe it's funny I never asked it before this.*

"Why did you think I'd be different from those other guys you tried to help?" I demanded. "How could you be so sure?"

"I wasn't." Mr. S looked at me thoughtfully. "How much do you know about those other boys? Why haven't you asked any of this before?"

"Why?" I insisted. "Why did you trust me to come work for you and live with you when you didn't know a thing about me?"

"Why did you agree to work for me and live out at the farm?" he countered.

"I didn't have any choice at the time," I replied.

"Neither did I," he answered. "Neither did I." And he wouldn't say any more.

Twenty

In Search Of

We followed Highway 62 east until we intersected with 63 north. In Missouri, we turned onto State 19 and took that all the way into Alton. From there we could veer east again on 160 toward Many Springs or continue north on 19 until we reached Greer. We decided to visit the site of the old mill at Greer on Eleven Point River. Mr. S's mother had died coming home from Greer's Mill. After that, everything had changed for him. It seemed appropriate our time trip into the past should start at Greer's Mill.

The mill stood at the summit of a good-sized hill. A rock foundation supported the gray, weather-beaten, two-story structure. The mill works were housed in the building, but the water wheel and spring were several hundred yards down the hill. The continuous steel cable which stretched from the mill house down to the water wheel had transmitted power for year-after-year until the mill was shut down just before World War I.

Listening to the distant underground stream bubbling noisily into the Eleven Point River, I could almost imagine the millstone turning slowly, just as it had years before. On that private TV screen in my head, there were buckboards loaded with bulky sacks of grain rolling up the winding trail leading to Greer's Mill. I could picture ladies in long dresses, their faces hidden by frilly sunbonnets, calling to one another as they herded children toward the grassy slopes of the hill. Milling day would have been a social time for the women, a chance to visit with friends and exchange news.

I wondered if the day Mr. S's mother died had started out warm and sunny like this one, but then I remembered she had died in October. Just thinking about her made me sad. I figured Mr. S was feeling pretty low, too. It would be hard to go back to a place that held such painful memories. I glanced over at him, trying to read his thoughts, but he took no notice of me. He was looking around, testing his memory for details. Whenever his eyes rested on a particular stone or tree or other landmark, he paused and smiled. Evidently, his memory served him well. I was glad we had made the trip.

Mr. S wasn't ready to leave until midafternoon. I was so hungry I ate all the way to Alton. Mr. S ate a sandwich with me, but because we were still hungry, we decided to get some ice cream in town.

Alton seemed like a nice place to live. In lots of ways, it reminded me of Berryville. There was a little shopping area downtown where ladies in cotton shirtwaist dresses strolled. Canopies of huge trees shaded the narrow side streets. Children yelled across the road to one another and stopped to stare at our car. There was a Super Scoop ice cream stand not far from an abandoned, ugly brick building. Only one other car was parked in the gravel lot, an odd deal since the weather was so hot and humid. Once we stepped up to the window, though, I had no trouble understanding the lack of customers.

The girl who waited on us looked like she was the only one who ever ate any of the ice cream. Rolls of fat strained against the seams of her dirty white uniform. A crumpled cap topped a stringy mop of hair which was pulled back into a loose ponytail. As she slid the glass pane that separated us, a cold draft from the noisy air conditioner hit me in the stomach and made a detour to my knees.

"Yeah? Kin I he'p ya?"

Mr. S and I studied the menu, trying to choose something this beaut couldn't screw up.

"Hurry up, wouldja? The cold air's gettin' out."

I settled on a vanilla cone and Mr. S ordered a frozen chocolate shake. My order was a disaster. The ice cream had a metallic taste as though it had been sitting in the machine for about a year and was on the verge of turning into metal itself. I looked over to see if Mr. S had given up on his shake. Surprisingly, he was wolfing it down like a man in the desert would guzzle water. I could only shake my head. Mr. S must have an iron stomach. Maybe that metallic ice cream was just the ticket for him.

He let me drive to Many Springs while he polished off the shake. I'll admit the trip's excitement had worn off a little for me. I guess I thought our "going back" would be like war heroes going home to a tickertape parade. There should be friends to meet you and talk about old times, not some heavyweight girl with a voice like a hog caller serving metallic ice cream through a greasy window.

Mr. S was of a different mind, though. He talked about the home place where his family lived before the accident at the mill. After Mr. S's mother died, his dad had to sell the only home he'd ever known, and Mr. S was shipped out to any relative or family friend who was willing to take him in. He vaguely remembered the family that moved in after the Skipworths left, but he doubted they'd still be around.

Many Springs wasn't at all what I'd imagined. I was expecting old and small. I wasn't expecting a ghost town. There were three or four paved streets, and I guessed all of five families lived within the town limits. If we had blinked twice, we would have missed everything.

Following Mr. S's directions, I kept driving until we reached an old farmhouse. Mr. S motioned for me to stop. We sat silently for a few minutes, staring at the weathered house with its wide, sagging porch.

"My dad hated leaving. This was home. It was our home." He paused before continuing. "When Mother died, though, he didn't have any choice. Those were hard times, and he tried to keep us together. He did. It was too much for him, though. *We* were too much for him," Mr. S said. He seemed to mentally shake himself, like a dog shedding water. When he spoke again, there was a detached, almost impersonal tone to his voice. "The family that bought the place knew Dad pretty well. Wonder what's happened to them."

"Maybe the people who live here now could give you some information," I suggested. "Why don't we check it out?"

We climbed the wide front steps leading to a covered porch. Through the screen door, we heard a radio playing Freddie Fender's "Before the Next Teardrop Falls." An electric fan whirred somewhere inside. Mr. S knocked on the door and stood patiently waiting for an answer. His hands were clasped behind his back the way they always are when he is thinking. When no one answered, he knocked again, and then, uncharacteristically, leaned his face against the screen, his hands cupped to frame his eyes. "Hello," he called. "Is anyone home?"

"Guess no one's here," he concluded after a few moments. "I suppose there's no point in waiting." I could hear the disappointment in his voice.

"Maybe we could do something else for awhile and then try back later," I suggested. "Isn't there anything else around here you'd like to see or do?"

"Well," he thought for a moment. "Used to be, there was a swallow-hole around these parts. Seems I remember one not far from here. It was always a mystery to me such a hole could just open up out in the middle of nowhere," he said. "I guess the roof of a cave collapsed. When the swallowing was done, that sinkhole was maybe fifty feet deep in the center and at least three hundred feet across. My dad always told me to be careful but it amazed me as a boy. I wonder if we could find that ol' hole?"

I didn't really understand all the fuss. I mean, it would be pretty hard to lose a hole so wide and deep. Not that I thought a hole in the ground was particularly exciting, but it obviously meant a lot to Mr. S. I planned to play along no matter what. After all, it was my idea to take this little time trip anyway.

As we walked to the Chevy, Mr. S pointed in the general direction of the Pacific Ocean and talked about an old road he remembered might lead us to the sinkhole. Armed with that meager information, we went in search of a memory.

Looking for that hole turned out to be the best part of the trip. We lost our way about seven times. We were given wrong directions at least twice that often. But we did get a chance to talk, and it was almost like we were pioneers starting out to conquer the wilderness.

Mr. S said the old swallow-hole had been fascinating because, aside from the Ozark Mountains themselves, it was the biggest geological feature he had ever seen as a boy. He remembered standing at the edge of the hole and looking at the earth far below. The banks were all rock and red clay, and a stream ran at the bottom. He remembered wintering the family's hogs in the shelter of its banks where they fed on wild artichokes, Jewish artichokes, he called them. "Those 'chokes were a lot like a potato," he explained. "The fleshy part grew underground, and they sure cut down on the feed bills."

We must have covered half of Missouri before we found the hole. Like everything else from Mr. S's past, it had changed over the years. The banks were thick with trees and scraggly shrubs that grew right up the slopes so that just by standing at the top, it was hard to tell how deep the thing really was.

Even though the afternoon sun waned, Mr. S and I decided to trek down to the basin floor. The trees were even more dense than they looked from the top, and the tangled undergrowth forced us to detour many times before we finally reached the bottom. Long scratches, tattoos from the tall, thorny bushes, crisscrossed our arms, and pesky little black gnats buzzed around our ears and in our noses. On the way down, I accidentally slipped, flopping my ankle over and twisting it. At first I wasn't bothered, but by the time we stopped at the bottom, it was throbbing pretty badly.

We were practically ready to drop from exhaustion and hunger by the time we struggled back to the top. My ankle shot pulsing waves of pain with every step, and I had to sit down and rest several times before continuing the climb. After three or four times of planting my rear on the ground, I couldn't decide which was worse—putting up with the pain in my ankle or with the chiggers and seed ticks that bit at my ankles and found their way up my pant legs and under my shirt.

I was limping badly when we got to the car. Mr. S helped me into the back seat and propped my leg up to relieve the pressure. I knew I'd be okay if I could just get a wrap on my foot and some food in my stomach. The only thing that bothered me was I probably couldn't find any place around Many Springs that would sell an elastic bandage, or even aspirin for that matter. Too, I didn't know where we were planning to spend the night. The prospect of curling up on the back seat of the Chevy didn't do much for my disposition.

My own problems made me less observant than usual. Mr. S was puffing and wheezing after settling me in the Chevy, but I didn't let that register then. Funny I remember those details now. He shuffled more slowly than ever around to the driver's side, his left shoulder dipping down awkwardly with each step he took. With considerable effort, he opened the car door and practically fell into the front seat. He sat, resting his hands on the steering wheel, and tried to regulate his ragged breathing.

It took several minutes for him to catch his breath before he could shake his head. "Just getting old," he mumbled. "I get so darn tired so fast anymore."

Mr. S put the car in gear and we headed back in the general direction we had come. I think we lost our way even more often than when we were looking for the sinkhole. Mr. S wasn't really paying attention to the route we had traveled, and I only confused him by sticking my head up and giving directions every so often.

To complicate things, my ankle had ballooned, maybe to twice its regular size. Bright purple streaks ran through the big bruise on the outside of my ankle, and the skin had taken on a sickly shine. "I think I need to head to the emergency room," I said. "Maybe I broke something. Do you think we can see a doctor as soon as we get home?"

Mr. S surprised me. "Just for a sprained ankle, you'd run off to the hospital?" He shook his head. "We'll rub a little liniment into it when we get back to the farm. Your foot will be fine. I don't see any need to consult a doctor."

"Mr. S, I think I need crutches, at least until the swelling goes down and I can squeeze my foot into my sneakers again," I protested.

"We need to get you back home," he agreed, "but we'll see about the hospital."

The ride home seemed longer than it should, mostly because Mr. S had to drive all the way. I think I was lucky to be lying down in the back seat. I didn't have to see all the almost-accidents, and from the honking horns and our swerving Chevy, there must have been several. By the time we drove through Berryville close to midnight, the town was deserted and dark, and I was surprised when Mr. S drove straight to the hospital.

In the emergency waiting room, Mr. S completed all the paperwork before a couple of nurses ushered me into an examining room. One of them called over her shoulder to Mr. S as he took a seat in the waiting room. "You're certainly welcome to wait with Ross in the examining room, sir."

"Thank you, no." Mr. S almost barked at the nurse. He sat down as though he couldn't care less about me. Even if they had amputated my foot, he would have sat there, calm as you please. I wondered why he went all ballistic every time someone in a white coat came within fifty feet of him, but then I remembered his wife, Faye, and how doctors couldn't save her.

My ankle wasn't broken, and I hadn't torn any ligaments. That was the good part. The bad part was the sprain was so severe the doctor said I couldn't go out for football.

"Sometimes a sprain takes longer to heal than a broken bone," he told me. "And you didn't do this job halfway." The doctor set me up with crutches, painkillers, and some of those freezable cold packs. If I elevated my foot as much as possible over the next two days, then I might be able to start school with everyone else on Tuesday. The doctor suggested I have someone help carry my books around from class to class. Naturally, I thought of Sara. I planned to call her and arrange things as soon as I could.

It was good to be home and plant myself in one spot and, I'll admit, once he left the clinic, Mr. S was the picture of concern. He made sure I was comfortable, brought me pillows and snacks, and told me he'd get me anything I wanted. All I had to do was ask.

"There is one thing," I said. "Could you bring me that book you've been wanting me to read? I can't think of a better time to get started." Mr. S had been pushing a couple of his favorite books at me lately. I figured I could skim at least one of them so we could talk. He'd be satisfied, and I'd get the reading out of the way before the required stuff from school assignments started piling up.

His face lit up like a Christmas tree as he hustled off to find it. He was back in no time with *The Bible Unmasked*, a thick volume that looked like it had survived the book burning in Hitler's day. It was so worn, in fact, I was afraid the binding would crumble in my hands. With a sigh, I started reading.

I can lose myself in a book, and this one made me think about ideas I'd never considered much before. The book spelled out Mr. S's philosophy about religion. I'd heard him say more people have been killed in holy wars in the name of God than in any natural disaster on the face of the earth. He shook his head when he talked about the Crusades.

"Would a good God, a just God, approve of the killing and plundering that supposedly happened to 'save the masses?'" Mr. S had often wondered aloud. "And look at the bloodshed in Ireland... all over religious differences. I'll never understand why people want to skewer each other in holy wars. What's holy about that?" he criticized. "If fighting that kind of war is the only way to be saved, then I guess I'll be damned."

I didn't think Mr. S was headed for hell, though. Even though he said he didn't believe in any kind of organized religion, he was probably the most moral person I'd ever known. He was generous and trusting, he seemed to always look for the good in people, and he lived by his own high standards. He was honest with himself and everyone he met. I had a feeling if there ever was a day of reckoning, the pearly gates would swing wide for Mr. S while I'd be lucky to sneak in the back way through the servants' entrance.

I mean, I had been in trouble most of my life. If someone looked at me cross-eyed, that was reason enough to pick a fight. I would lie, even when the truth would have served just as well or better, and if I could get ahead at someone else's expense, then so be it. Sure, I had been baptized (the Greers, one of my many foster families, had insisted upon it as a condition of their taking me in), and I attended compulsory church services at The Cedars. But truth be told, I only prayed to God when I was trying to broker a deal. He was a silent four-leaf clover, a good luck charm to tip the scales when the odds weren't in my favor.

Maybe Mr. S proclaimed to be an atheist, but he did believe in a "higher power." He said he found divinity in the miracle of nature. Sunsets ringed in golden halos held him spellbound, and majestic Ozark landscapes humbled him. As he watched patterns of life play out their cyclic dramas on the stage of his farm, he bowed to their undeniable power.

"The strong survive, the clever adapt, and the weak die," he intoned. "It's the way of the world. Death doesn't play favorites. That's why your actions on earth are so important. This is your one chance to get it right."

Frankly, the more I thought about it, the more I hoped I'd merit more than one chance to "get it right." My track record hadn't been so hot most of my life, and I could use the leverage of an all-knowing being waiting in the wings, willing to forgive my shortcomings.

Even though I just skimmed some of the chapters, I finished most of *The Bible Unmasked.* Mr. S and I had a healthy debate, agreeing to disagree on some points, both of us satisfied to have had a sounding board, and neither of us needing to convert the other.

Luckily, we had the foresight to shelve the book before the social worker from the State Department came to visit.

Twenty-one

Scrutiny

We had been expecting the social worker. When the court granted the interlocutory decree, the judge gave us a timeline of events so we could prepare for the home visits. At least, we *thought* we were ready for the home visits. All by himself, Mr. S cleaned house and fussed over the yard so carefully it looked like it had been trimmed with his barber's scissors. I dressed more neatly than I had all summer, and Mr. S was sharp in a crisp white shirt and his best tie. We waited for the social worker in nervous silence. When she finally came, driving a spotless black Ford Fairlane, I knew we were in trouble.

She was wearing a dress that wasn't wrinkled or rumpled in the least, even though she'd driven all the way from Little Rock in the middle of one of the hottest September days on record. Her manner, brisk and businesslike, indicated she was used to holding a position of authority. Even Geraldine, after one sniff at the social worker's heels, whimpered and sidled away, her tail between her legs. If we were nervous before, Mr. S and I were ready for electroshock treatments by the time we worked up enough courage to open the door.

"I'm Miss Esther Landon," she said. "I'm expected, I believe." She walked in without allowing either of us to stammer out some false word of welcome. Seating herself on the sofa at the far end of the living room, she surveyed the room with critical eyes. Her stare settled on Mr. S's endless bookshelves.

"An extensive library," she observed.

"Mr. Skipworth reads all the time," I explained, too eagerly, "and he encourages me to read, too." At her continued silence, I felt compelled to elaborate, stupidly, "He's a really smart man, …really."

"I see," she responded. "Well, let's get right to the matter at hand. I've reviewed the petition and decree issued by Judge Carter. I've also contacted a number of the references you listed on the original application and checked into young Mr. Benedict's juvenile records from The Cedars. You have inordinate support, apparently, for this adoption to proceed." She paused for a moment before continuing. "Buried as I am by the number of more *suitable* adoptions underway that need processing, I suppose we should begin." We responded with stunned, blank stares, but Miss Landon seemed not to notice.

"I assume you are ready to proceed with the interview," she said. From a severe black briefcase she produced several official-looking papers. Miss Landon poised her pencil, sharpened to a fine point, above the first question.

And so it went. She mercilessly filled her questionnaire with neat, even handwriting, never stopping to erase a mistake or pausing to consider her choice of words. Our responses never seemed to please her. For that matter, they didn't anger or upset her, either. She was merely indifferent. Our case wasn't worthy of praise or put-downs in her estimation. It just wasn't important enough to merit serious consideration. I wondered how many cases she had ruthlessly handled, not caring she practically had the power of life and death over the people she investigated. I wanted to tell the old hag where to stuff her opinions, but through the whole ordeal, Mr. S answered all her questions honestly in a pleasant, quiet voice.

I held my breath when Miss Landon asked about religious affiliations, but Mr. S's answer, "None," didn't even elicit a raised eyebrow. After a grueling session that lasted almost an hour, Miss Landon was ready to ask the last required question. There was a full page of blank space for the answer.

"As a prospective adoptive parent, what do you feel is the most important aspect in providing a good home?" You could have written reams and never given an answer the State Department would find acceptable. I wondered how Mr. S would handle this one. His face took on that glassy look he always gets when he's about to lecture on religion or the lessons to be learned in life. Then Mr. S looked straight at Miss Landon and told her to write his answer, word-for-word.

"Young people like Ross are the promise of the future. You need to train them right, train them to know about hard work, about how to do things with their heads and their hands. If you can do that, then you've done the best a parent can do." Mr. S smiled at Miss Landon for the first time since she arrived.

"That's all?" she asked. "Most prospective parents wish to comment about developing morals or the value of an education and..." It was the only sentence Miss Landon never finished.

"I believe I just did." Mr. S smiled again, clearly pleased with himself. "If there are no more questions, I'll show you to your car. Ross and I have work to do today."

He rose, politely waited for Miss Landon to follow suit, and gallantly offered her his arm as he led her to her car. Heat waves shimmered above the Fairlane, and I thought with pleasure the car's interior would be hotter than an oven. I waved goodbye to Miss Landon's back, and felt better than I had all day.

The euphoria at her departure didn't last very long, but for a brief moment, neither one of us cared what recommendations old Leadhead Landon would make to the State Department.

"Why should we worry about a woman who comes to a battle of wits only half-equipped?" Mr. S said, laughing.

It took me a full minute to understand Mr. S, in his gentlemanly way, had just called Miss Landon a half-wit.

Twenty-two

Judgment Day

My injured ankle kept me from playing football, but not from being a team manager. All the scuz jobs came to me—picking up dirty towels, keeping the water bottles filled, being a gofer for the coach, filling the equipment bags for road trips. Even so, I was on the field every day with the players, and during games I strutted around on the sidelines wearing Berryville Bobcats purple and gold. Some of the team members nicknamed me "Ross the Boss" which was eventually shortened to "Boss." Practically everyone at High called me that, so—in a way—not being able to go out for the squad was almost better than being a super jock. I was invited to all the team parties, the cheerleaders and I were on friendly terms, and my brains remained comfortably in my head instead of being spilled on the field with every play.

After the first few weeks of school, my classes settled into a familiar pattern. I sheepishly admitted to Sara I went *slightly* overboard before the term started. "Maybe buying all those supplies was overkill," I confessed.

"Duh! Ya think?" she chided. "After all, school will always be school."

My grades were okay in everything but chemistry. As Sara predicted, I was flunking miserably, right along with every other sophomore and even a few of the repeat upperclassmen.

Still, I think Mr. S and I were equally pleased with my performance. I was doing better than I ever had at The Cedars, a fact which Mr. S bragged about to the old timers in the town square every chance he got. My textbooks fascinated Mr. S, especially the ones for World Civilizations. Many nights he'd ask about my assignments on the Greek city states and the Roman Empire, or he'd try to find one of his books about the sea-going Phoenicians or the Moors of northern Africa. In fact, it wasn't unusual for me to have to leave for school an hour or so before my first class because I hadn't finished my homework in my other subjects the night before.

I liked sitting in the library on those mornings. The librarian got in the habit of kidding me about my early morning appearances. She kept asking if I planned on finishing high school in one year instead of three.

Every time she asked, I laughed just like it was the most clever thing I'd ever heard in my life. Then I would go behind the stacks next to the short story collection and try to concentrate on the homework I hadn't finished. Most of the time I stuck with the assigned work, but every once in awhile I'd just pick a book off the shelf and read until I lost track of time. Too often, I'd end up being late for my first hour class—chemistry, no less.

Anyway, September melted into October and then November. Before I knew it, football season was over. The weather, still warm for so late in the year, allowed Mr. S and me to get a lot of work done around the farm. One weekend in particular, the roof needed to be sealed tight next to the chimney before winter set in. Mr. S and I climbed up on the deck over the garage and eased over the peak of the roof. I carried a bucket of tar and Mr. S carried the brushes. It was late in the afternoon. A cool breeze was blowing and the work was almost fun. Geraldine even followed us up onto the roof and padded around behind us as we worked. She seemed as at home on top of the house as she did playing guard dog in the yard below.

Earlier that day I had mowed the lawn and trimmed the shrubs for what I hoped was the last time that year. Mr. S wanted everything picture perfect because Vernon and Jorita were coming for the Thanksgiving holiday. When Mr. S told me about their upcoming visit, I didn't even have to pretend I was happy. Ever since the scene in August, I'd been hoping for a chance to work things out face-to-face with Jorita. Maybe we could patch up our differences and make everything right again. I think that's the only real trouble Mr. S and I ever had. He loved Jorita and he was loyal to me. Our falling out probably tore him in half. It's kind of ironic you can be hurt most by people you love most.

Thanksgiving was still a couple of weeks away. I had plenty of time to practice what I'd say to Jorita. In the meantime, Mr. S and I had to psych up for another friendly visit from the ever-lovely Miss Landon, our social worker. She had three mandatory interviews scheduled, and the second date was already looming. After the first fiasco, I'd rather have worn a dress and competed in the Pillsbury Bake-Off than face that witch again.

Miss Landon obviously felt the same about us because she never showed for the interview. That Sunday afternoon crept by more slowly than any other in my memory. Mr. S and I sat in the living room waiting for Miss Landon's hearse to pull into the driveway. As the minutes ticked away and her lateness became desertion, Mr. S and I could only guess what Miss Landon's absence meant for the success of the adoption. We couldn't decide whether I should start packing my bags or plan a "Congratulate Me, I've Just Been Adopted" party.

After I'd mumbled, "She could've at least called," and Mr. S had repeated, "No news is good news," for the hundredth time, we changed into our work clothes and went out to inspect the cattle. We had been corn feeding one heifer for butchering and Mr. S wanted to check on her especially. Maybe, I thought, someone at the State Welfare Department finally got wise and was fattening Miss Landon for butchering, too. Other than that, I didn't give her any more of my time.

Early Monday morning, we woke to the sound of screeching tires. Someone had rounded the corner just east of Mr. S's property going too fast for the turn and had lost control. A green Chrysler had stopped nose end into the field next to the barn across the road, but not before it had plowed through two fence posts, dragging barbed wire all the way. With a lot of grunting and shoving, we managed to help the driver get the Chrysler back on the shoulder, but the fence was hopeless. We'd have to drive new posts and stretch the wire back in place, a full day's work for both of us. Mr. S didn't like the idea of my missing school, but there wasn't any other choice. We had about twenty head in that field, and it was a sure bet some of them would wander out on the highway if we waited to fix the fence. Mr. S called the attendance office at High to set the record straight. We ate a breakfast of cold cereal and untoasted bread before we got to work.

Mr. S wasn't satisfied with the repair job until well past lunch time. Even in the cool weather, we must have sweat away ten pounds apiece. To add the crowning blow, water backed up in the shower when I tried to clean up. We worked for thirty minutes with the plunger, but that didn't help. The drain out to the septic pool was clogged and we had to dig it out to get the water running clear again.

Mr. S and I pulled on rubber work boots and headed toward the culvert west of the house. The weeds were thick and the grass so high we couldn't even find the drainage ditch for quite a while. By accident, Mr. S stepped in the basin, muck sloshing up over his feet. I dug a trough to shovel all the sludge away, about the nastiest job in the world. But at least the water drained when Mr. S turned on the spigots full force.

By the time I had showered and changed, I was starving. Neither of us was in the mood to cook something. In a moment of weakness, Mr. S suggested we drive into town for a sandwich and some onion rings. Since it was the first and only time we ever went out for dinner, I agreed almost faster than he offered.

We ate like pigs. Mr. S had a foot-long chili dog, I had a double-decker cheeseburger, and we each polished off an order of onion rings and two chocolate malts. For dessert, I ordered a hot fudge sundae and Mr. S had a slice of lemon meringue pie. We couldn't seem to help gorging ourselves, but we paid for our gluttony. I groaned and Mr. S belched all the way home, and our stomachs were tighter than a tick's. I could hardly remember a time when Mr. S hadn't watched the late news, but that night, neither of us could have cared if the world ended. We changed our clothes and fell into bed. Sleep was priority one.

No matter how hard I tried to keep my aching body in bed Tuesday morning, Mr. S. wouldn't allow me a day's rest before sending me back to school. I struggled into my jeans and a shirt, gulped some orange juice, and was ready to leave with Mr. S. On the way into town, I was a little disappointed Mr. S didn't make over me and sympathize just a little. All he said was, "Thanks for your help," and that was it.

I left Mr. S at the shop and walked over to school. I was early, as usual, but that gave me time to catch up on some of the work I'd missed. It took will power to stay awake during my classes, especially since the weather was so gloomy. The clouds, dark and thick, blackened the middle of the day, and I was reminded winter wouldn't be put off any longer. A steady rain fell all day, and the temperature fell with the rain. By the time school was out, I was wishing I'd worn a heavy sweatshirt.

Partly to warm up and partly because I just liked picking up the mail, I stopped by the post office on my way to the shop. There was the usual assortment of junk mail and one official looking envelope with a familiar return address:

Child Welfare Division
State Department of Public Welfare
Capital Mall
Little Rock, Arkansas

This must be the reason Landon the Leper hadn't shown up for the second interview, I thought. Even though the letter was officially addressed to Mr. S, I figured we were in this thing together. As I tore open the envelope, my hands shook from more than the cold.

> *Mr. Skipworth:*
>
> *This letter is to inform you of the resolution regarding your petition to adopt Ross A. Benedict. Although the proceedings typically take six months to complete, the State Department has reviewed your situation. We believe special consideration is merited.*
>
> *Under separate mailing, you will receive official notice regarding the decision by the State Department to remove Esther Landon as the social worker handling your case file. I regret this information would not have reached you prior to the second of your scheduled home visitations, and I apologize*

for any inconvenience this might have caused. Under other circumstances, another counselor would be assigned to complete the interview process, but considerations unique to your case have overridden that need.

While I do not wish to engage in specifics, let me simply say Miss Landon's report was uncharacteristically biased against your petition for adoption. In a matter of such weighty consequence, an unfounded predisposition on the part of our case worker is unacceptable. Contradictory to her report, we have on file numerous affidavits from The Cedars administrative team, Sheriff Herschel Stoner, and authorities from Berryville Senior High School. All the aforementioned persons have submitted documentation verifying Ross's social and emotional well-being since he has been in your care. That fact, when coupled with Ross's age, justifies a more immediate look at your petition for adoption.

Based upon our findings, we are hereby waiving the usual six-month waiting period. This department recommends the proposed adoption be processed with all due speed. As soon as Judge Carter can schedule a final date for the hearing, the necessary papers

can be signed and recorded.
I extend to you and Ross my most sincere congratulations.

Linwood Settle
State Department of Public Welfare

~ * ~

I was going to be Mr. S's son.

I tore out of the post office clutching the letter in my hand and ran across the middle of the square toward the shop. As I passed the fountain, I stopped and laughed out loud. The basin was empty now, drained and cleaned and ready for winter. I stood there until the rain drenched me through to my skin.

Mr. S was in his chair when I burst through the double doors. His opened paper was spread across his lap. His hands hung limply on either side of his barber chair. His head was tilted to one side against the headrest, and his mouth was wide open, its usual position when he slept.

"Mr. S, wake up! Your *son* has brought the mail for you." I grinned and waited for a reaction, but there was nothing.

"Mr. S? Did you hear me? Mr. S?" I shook his shoulder. His head fell forward and his chin sort of bounced on his chest and was still. His bifocals slid down to the tip of his nose.

"Mr. S, please wake up. You'll want to read this. It's what we've waited to hear. Please, Mr. S. Please."

He didn't answer. He wouldn't ever answer.

The tears rolling down my cheeks partly blurred my vision, but not enough to block the sight of Mr. S sitting lifelessly in his chair, cheating us both. He was everywhere I looked, his image reflected over and over in the mirrors that lined the room. He was my father. And he was dead.

That's when I lost it. I doubled up my fists and—slowly at first—I started pounding away at the mirrors. I kept punching the glass again and again... faster and faster... harder and harder and harder.

When Sheriff Stoner found me, I was standing by Mr. S's chair, surrounded by shattered glass. Blood was dripping from my torn knuckles, running down my fingers and making unusual splatter marks on Mr. S's floor. I was staring at my hands, but I couldn't feel them. Honest to God, I couldn't. All I could think about was my hands were stained red once before. Only then, the stains weren't blood.

Epilogue

Looking Glass, Present Day

The glass of the old barbershop window felt cool against my forehead, but my palms were plastered to the surface, suctioned there with sweat and remembrance. I felt captive, unwilling to stay, unable to go.

"Hey. What's up? Is everything okay?" I stepped back to see the reflection of a young man, maybe fourteen or fifteen, staring at me from his vantage on the sidewalk. "Did you lose something in there?" he asked.

Released from an invisible pull, I turned from the past to look at the boy. "Yes. Yes, I did, but it was a long time ago. A very long time ago."

"I know the people who run this place. Maybe you could call the owner," he suggested. He peered through the glass intently, his hands cupped around his face to lessen the sun's glare. "Whatever you lost might still be there."

I turned back to the window, startled to see myself reflected in the glass. Gone was the wiry boy with bloodied knuckles and tear-streaked face. In his place a middle-aged man with thinning hair stared back at me. What did he see? Did he approve of what I had become?

After Mr. S died, the county didn't know what to do with me. I spent that first awful night in the hospital. Doctors bandaged my hands, gave me antibiotics, painkillers, and sedatives, but there was no prescription to heal my heart. Loss and rage can be shoved aside, given a pink slip for a short time, but those insistent twins always want to kick in the door and take up permanent residence. I played host to them for a long time, and we kept exclusive company.

I had no other choice but to go back to The Cedars. Not surprisingly, that stint didn't last long. Within six weeks I managed to land myself in the juvenile detention center in Eureka Springs. At some point the authorities contacted Jorita, and—to her credit—she offered to take me in. I didn't want her charity, and said so. I didn't want to need anybody.

In March, I celebrated my sixteenth birthday in a locked room under suicide watch. My only visitors were social workers, shrinks, and my court-appointed child advocate. Occasionally, I'd get letters from Jorita. I never opened them.

She was persistent, though, and still is. One day, early in June, the child advocate told me to pack my things. I had been enrolled in the Military Academy in Mexico, Missouri. My tuition was courtesy of Jorita Skipworth Jones.

I may have been too little to play football for Coach Rothrock at Berryville High, but the military school didn't care how I was packaged. They put me in uniform, clothed my anger in a jacket of discipline, and helped my spit-polished boots regain footing on a path I thought no longer navigable, a path cleared by a steadfast old man, unwavering compass in hand.

It took me three years to earn my diploma. I had lost so much of my sophomore year when Mr. S died I had to repeat that grade. But slowly, painfully, I found something of myself—something of Mr. S—that had survived. I did well enough by my senior year to earn a diploma denoting academic distinction. Jorita and Vernon both came for graduation. We were cordial if not comfortable.

Several colleges accepted my application for admission, but I chose to study at the University of Arkansas. Jorita insisted on supplementing my scholarship. "It's what Daddy would have wanted," she said. I worked for grant-in-aid money at the library at night, and on the weekends I took a part time job at the rec center. My favorite days were when the center rented facilities for family parties. I'd set up the volleyball nets or organize a game of basketball for the little kids, who generously let me play.

I decided on a major in education with emphasis on the earth sciences. Whether I had a natural affinity, or my interest was fueled by some vestige of Mr. S's influence, I can't say, but I've been at the same high school in Little Rock for my whole career.

Jorita, still sharp in old age, keeps an album of the pictures I send her. Every year I take my students on a field trip to the Ouachita Mountains for lab work, and we pose in goofy postures, hamming it up for the camera. Even though I've extended many invitations, she has never visited me in Little Rock. She could not drive here without passing through Berryville, and that she will not do. Within a year of Mr. S's death, she had sold the farm and the shop. Her memories, she says, are neatly catalogued in her head, and she doesn't need to revisit a place to recall what happened there, both the good and the bad.

Until now, neither had I.

"Did you hear me, Mister?" The boy beside me interrupted my thoughts. "I asked if whatever you lost might still be in there."

I imitated his posture, leaning again against the window, my hands framing my face. "You know, I think you're right. I didn't lose it at all. Even after all this time, I can see it, plain as day."

The boy pulled out his cell phone and began keying

in numbers. "If we can get a guy out here to open the building…"

"Thanks," I assured him, "but you don't need to disturb anyone right now. I can come back later. I can definitely come back."

Acknowledgments

The Skipworth Summer is possible only because of the real *Luther Skipworth*, my grandfather. Events in his life inspired this novel, but it is a work of fiction. So, what is real? The information about Skip's early years is completely factual. His mother did die when he was 10 years old in an accident as the family returned from the grist mill in Many Springs, Missouri. In fact, the obituary in the novel is quoted exactly from the death notice as it appeared in 1910. A young, motherless boy, Skip was shuttled to multiple families. Denied the opportunity to attend school beyond the third grade, Skip valued education above all else. As such, he was tireless in his pursuit of knowledge. He prized his extensive collection of books, proudly embossing each title page with a seal noting his ownership. He and his bride, *Faye Lewis Skipworth*, worked as barber and beautician in the building on the corner of Church Street in Berryville, Arkansas. Artifacts from his many years as a barber are still on display at the Pioneer Heritage Museum, and the curators there were most gracious in sharing information from their archives.

Skip did lose his wife in 1951, and details of Faye's death are factual, but he did remarry and was survived by his second wife, Phenie. In the matter of Skip's death, fiction was far kinder than reality. Instead of passing quietly away in the barber shop he loved, Skip suffered a debilitating stroke. Complications from the stroke claimed his life a year later. Ross Benedict is completely fictional, but Skip did at one point want very much to take in two boys to live and work on the farm. My knowledge of that intention provided the "What if" that is the fountainhead for all story tellers.

The novel originally was written as a gift to my own children, Skip's great-grandchildren, because I wanted to capture for them the grandfather I so idolized and whom they would never really know. I owe my mother, Jorita, unending gratitude for graciously allowing me to tell this story in which she plays a large part and for her permission to invent or alter details of Skip's and her life for the sake of the narrative. My oldest sister Karen, with her absolute recall of almost everything, helped validate memories that comprise the chapters about the family's visit to the farm. My friend Lin Settle provided invaluable insights and suggestions through multiple revisions. Foremost, however, my husband Rick was patient and supportive throughout the entire process, uncomplaining as I spent countless hours at the computer and ever confident that the story would sometime find a wider audience.

Meet

Jan Netolicky

Jan Netolicky is a retired language arts teacher who lives with her husband in Robins, IA.

*VISIT OUR WEBSITE
FOR THE FULL INVENTORY
OF QUALITY BOOKS*:

http://www.wings-press.com

*Quality trade paperbacks and downloads
in multiple formats,
in genres ranging from light romantic
comedy to general fiction and horror.
Wings has something
for every reader's taste.
Visit the website, then bookmark it.
We add new titles each month!*